LOVELACE FLATS

Jupiter Jones grew up on the north-west coasts of Cumbria and Lancashire. The first was wild and secretive, the second trashy and jaded; she loved them both. After a brief spell in London to complete a PhD in Spectatorial Embarrassment at Goldsmiths, she now lives in Wales and writes short and flash fictions. She is the winner of the Colm Tóibín International Prize (2018 and 2021) and her stories and flash have been published by *Aesthetica*, *Brittle Star*, Fish, Reflex Press, Scottish Arts Trust, and her novella-in-flash *The Death and Life of Mrs Parker* by Ad Hoc Fiction.

ALSO BY JUPITER JONES

The Death and Life of Mrs Parker

Lovelace Flats

Jupiter Jones

REFLEX PRESS

First published in 2022 by Reflex Press
Abingdon, Oxfordshire, OX14 3SY
www.reflex.press

A CIP catalogue record of this book is
available from the British Library.

ISBN: 978-1-914114-08-3

1 3 5 7 9 10 8 6 4 2

Printed and bound in Great Britain by
Imprint Digital, Upton Pyne, Exeter.

Cover image by Henry & Co.

www.reflex.press/lovelace-flats/

CONTENTS

Prologue: Medium-Rise, Medium-Density Hell

When they were first built, people said the Lovelace Flats were a dream: clean, modern, affordable. Then the wind changed, and they said the flats were bad: brutalist monstrosities built in the wrong place, out on the very edge of civilization.

Crime rates were high. Councillors with homes in the suburbs banged their fists on tables; something must be done. They blamed the police. The police blamed the lack of funding. Sociologists mapped the fracture and decline of communities. Alienation, they said. Criminologists scrutinized communal spaces and confirmed that crime was inevitable: we were rats in rat runs. Then someone blamed the architecture. The architect was already dead. Structural surveyors condemned the precast concrete slabs, and sometime later, theorists would coin the term sick building syndrome. The bold experiment in social engineering was a failure, a medium-rise, medium-density hell. There was isolation, depression, vandalism, gangs, drugs, litter, dog shit, truancy, intimidation, prostitution, ill health, decay, lawlessness, poverty, suicide.

No one on the council waiting list wanted to be housed at Lovelace, '*not there*' they said. Some flats were empty, boarded up, some were squatted – not by enterprising or politically motivated types – but by the dispossessed, a squalid substratum of hopelessness.

In January 1982, the City Council, scratching for revenue, decided to rent a small number of vacant flats to students from the polytechnic. It was arguably exploitative, perhaps cruel to billet clueless and inept neophytes in such a dystopia. But in that cold winter, it had a certain charm – it was a dystopia with underfloor heating – as if the flats were built directly over the fire pits of hell.

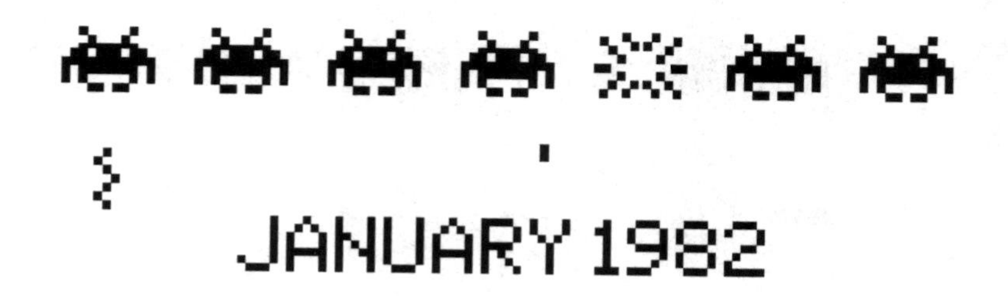

JANUARY 1982

'So, Would You Rather...' asks Woody, and the Game Begins

Petra, Woody, and Stan, with the keys in his pocket, caught the bus from the city centre out to Lovelace Flats. That first time, the journey was epic. The luggage rack was piled with rucksacks and art folders; Woody's saxophone and typewriter were taking up seat space.

It was bitterly cold. A freeze had gripped the East Midlands for weeks. Roads were treacherous with black ice, small birds perished in the trees, rough sleepers died in doorways. Petra was anxious about her coat. It was new, an impulse buy, and she was not sure she liked it as much as she had first thought. She sniffed the topaz silk lining, twirled her mouse-brown hair around her finger, and dreamed. Woody, a latter-day beatnik of unfocussed talent and cruel beauty, was smoking a Black Sobranie and scribbling in his notebook. Stan stared vacantly out of the window. Beyond the scratched and fogged glass, the amenities of city life, banks, nightclubs, taxis, bookshops, off-licences, health centres, takeaways, launderettes and even greengrocers were left behind as the bus stop-start growled in low gear up the Wells Road and into the badlands.

'My friend Louisa says we can have her old vacuum cleaner.'

Stan and Woody raised their eyebrows at Petra's unexpected token of domesticity.

~

Their destination, 40 Faraday Walk, Lovelace Flats, was vacant, unfurnished, and cheap. It was a long way from everything they thought mattered, but the underfloor heating was included in the rent, and that winter, it was so cold that Petra would gladly have bunked up with Lucifer himself. The night before, in the student union bar, the three of them had drunk to their new venture and agreed house rules.

'I don't want to have to see your scanty panties drying over the bath,' said Stan.

'You won't ever be that lucky,' said Petra. 'And no leaving your dirty books next to the loo.'

'Bog,' said Stan.

'Or lavatory, lav if you must—'

'Crapper.'

'I don't care what you call it so long as you don't expect me to clean it.'

'Alright, cut it out, you two,' said Woody. 'I've got a serious question. Would you rather... be totally safe or totally free?'

It was a question they were singularly ill-equipped to answer. Freedom or safety?

A choice between two abstract concepts they only half understood, and the antithesis of each, they hardly knew at all. Certainly not beyond the usual irksome restraints the middle classes imposed on their feckless offspring to curb their liberties, or in the case of danger, the lurking menace of men with sweets in their pockets. Nevertheless, they thought they knew.

'Free.'

'Free.'

'Yes! At last, we agree on something. Another one: Would you rather... be famous only during your lifetime, or only after you are dead? Come on, snap decision, what's it to be?'

'I'm going to say famous while I'm alive,' said Petra.

'And then forgotten when you're dead?' asked Woody, shrewishly, as if she had it wrong.

'Yeah, what will I care when I'm gone?'

'Stan, are you with her on this?'

Stanley looked from one to the other. 'Nope. I'd be happy to live in total obscurity so long as I can be massively famous when I'm dead – for my remarkable artwork, of course. More famous even than Le Corbusier or Cézanne.'

'Mmm, me too,' said Woody. 'I want to know I've left something behind, something permanent, a monument to my craft or sullen art. Otherwise, what's the point?'

'Well, live for now, have fun, isn't *that* the point?' said Petra.

'*Carpe diem*?'

'Ha! You're a bird in the hand, alright,' said Stan. 'Go on then, Slap, your turn.'

Two Tins of Kit-e-kat

Mr Kite puts on his overcoat and double locks the door of 81 Faraday Walk. He heads to Mr Khalil's shop for two tins of Kit-e-kat, one for Mungo, one for himself. Apart from the cat, he has no friends because he stinks of piss and is always disagreeable. He hears the sounds of gunshot and tyres screeching; his neighbours have their rented television on full blast. They are trying to drown out the sound of the baby crying in the flat below. It's colicky and fractious; its mother doesn't know what to do for the best – why would she? She is only fifteen. Mr Kite passes Libby Radford, anorexic, her mouth clamped shut to hide blackened teeth, loose in a cadaverous jaw. And Jean Banks carrying yesterday's paper. The scaremongering headline: TROUBLE BREWING IN SOUTH ATLANTIC.* She only wants it for the coupons. Jean is overweight and underloved; she misses her brother. He hanged himself two months back because of debt. His flat is now rented to a Vietnamese family who have no English, no work, and take turns with the shoes. Mr Hess from Babbage Walk was trying to teach them the lingo, but he's been diagnosed with throat cancer. His son Michael is in prison, due for parole any day now, fingers crossed, this time. Michael's erstwhile colleagues, Spud and Paulie, are still in business; they can get you most prescription drugs at reasonable prices and also speed or skag. Just ask. By

*'TROUBLE BREWING IN SOUTH ATLANTIC', *East Midlands Gazette*, 20 January 1982.

agreement, they don't now do puff. You should go to Leon for that. Or Skinny Pete. A kettle comes whistling to the boil. A dog yap-yap-yaps, 'shut the fuck up'. A radio blares. A door slams. Mr Kite passes Number 40, still empty, then Number 39 where Sycorax, the witch, still in her nightie, is hauling stinking black bags of rubbish out of the door. He turns left, down into the concrete stairwell. Hears sobbing at the bottom, puts up his collar, keeps walking. Two skinheads, Simon and Gareth, peacoated and clucking, hurry past him to the pub. An old settee has been fly-tipped on the pavement. Upholstered in orange velour and greasy in a way that makes Mr Kite nostalgic for antimacassars. Already, the settee is occupied. No one knows his name. He rants and raves and wears a close-fitting cap made out of tinfoil, 'fucking radiation,' he shouts. In the phone box, someone is losing an argument with their probation officer, social worker, money lender, or pimp. The short queue eavesdrops quite without shame. Mr Kite cuts through the dank underpass, sidesteps dogshit with a practiced manoeuvre, and reaches the erratically stocked shop with its graphited metal roller shutters and tatty striped awning. Here you can get pop, Pop-Tarts, popsicles, and popsocks, but not muesli. Vegetables are frozen or tinned. Vodka comes in two-litre plastic containers with photocopied labels. It's not on display. Just ask. Outside, sitting on the pavement, are two little skanks, their muzzles red-rashed with crusted scabs. They've just shoplifted a bag of smoky bacon crisps to go with their tin of Evo-Stik. Welcome to Lovelace Flats.

Home Improvements

As soon as she saw it, Petra was disappointed by the front door. The graffiti on the door.

DAVE. All in capitals, all in straight lines except the front of the D, which was two shallow arcs meeting at a point in the middle, making the shape of a finch's beak. Four-inch letters carved into the wood with a penknife, flick knife, switchblade, or whatever they kept in their pockets round there. She didn't like the colour of the paint either, a shabby blue, dull with oxidation, and she wanted it handsome and glossy, with new numbers and a brass knocker.

'No.' Stanley said no. 'You must not paint the door. It looks scuzzy, but it's a scuzzy neighbourhood, and it's best to fit in, or at least not to stand out.'

He had sandy coloured eyes, a wide mouth, and a practical streak. She made a face like a petulant child not allowed sweets. Stan folded his arms and laughed at her.

'If you want to improve the door, go to the hardware shop and buy a new lock. You have no idea who has lived here before us and who still has a key. You could come home to find the place has been burgled, ransacked and trashed, or they could let themselves in while you're asleep.'

'Dave,' she said. 'Maybe Dave lived here – maybe he'll come back.'

South Georgia, January 1982

With a legitimate contract to dismantle the old whaling station at Leith Harbour on South Georgia (seven hundred miles east of the Falkland Islands) Constantino Davidoff and a small party of Argentinians arrive to conduct a preliminary survey. They have the necessary clearance from the embassy in Buenos Aires but fail to report to the British base at Grytviken, thirty miles along the coast, to get their visas stamped.

So cold. This is a hollow, howling hell. The wind never stops. It shrieks around the station, chewing at loose panelling, moaning and muttering about dead whales and dead whalers. The chicanes of their bones funnelling dreams. I sleep in my earmuffs, and I have written to my mama asking her to send more gloves and coffee. I am so cold. The middle of summer, yet I am frozen to my marrow.

And fucking Constantino, think he is fucking God. All day, he is, 'Do this, Georg, do that.' Do it like this, do it faster, do it again. He can kiss my asshole.

Godforsaken fucking place. And for what? I ask: for fucking what? Is there not rusted metal enough back home in Buenos Aires?

The Nightjar

Nightjar: (Caprimulgidae) medium-sized nocturnal or crepuscular bird with long wings, short legs, and feet so dainty they are hardly any use at all for walking. Feeds on moths and other large flying insects. Colloquially called 'goatsuckers' due to folk tales that they were suckled by goats, which is ridiculous, obviously.

They changed the lock. The next day, they went to the second-hand furniture emporium behind the cinema. Three floors crammed with the detritus of other lives and the spoils of house clearance. Petra and Stan perused ironically, arm in arm, pretending to be an item. Stan, not unreasonably, said countless people had probably died in the old iron-framed bed Petra bought. He chose a divan, and she pointed out the unfortunate stain on the mattress. They agreed on a table and a set of folding chairs in utility brown, the seats and backs embossed with a pattern of crocodile skin like old luggage. Woody bought a desk, a rather beautiful but moth-eaten Persian rug, and an army camp bed.

Always part of some tenuous web of favours, Woody had borrowed a van to haul their new second-hand furniture home. They pulled up at the bottom of the flats and found the local kids hanging about to watch as they manhandled their gear up the piss-stinking stairwell and along the walkway. The kids hooted and hissed and offered to help, then fell about laughing like a pack of pantomime hyenas. After the students had lived at Lovelace a while, some of the hyenas would come close enough to take sweets or a cigarette from an outstretched hand. The older residents, however, were very much less accommodating. For them, the students would always be incomers, not 'from here'. They retained a sense of having been invaded.

Number 40 was a reverse layout with the front door at the top, kitchen and living room below that, and the bedrooms right at the bottom. The three students intended to get some carpet for the stairs; floorboards were not yet fashionable. Petra's friend Louisa and her girlfriend Harpo came bumping down with an old Electrolux vacuum cleaner.

'Hey! Your door was open,' called out Lou.

'You want to be careful leaving it open,' added Harpo.

'She's right,' said Lou. 'God knows what might get in. Cats at the very least, darling.'

Louisa and Harpo wore matching dungarees. Louisa was looking gorgeous; under hers, she wore a little white broderie anglaise top, and her hair was caught up in a floral bandana. Harpo was channelling more of a gulag look. And whilst Lou was chatty, Harpo brandished the chip on her shoulder like the stripes of an NCO. As vanguards of the student contingent, they had moved into a flat on Babbage Walk just two weeks earlier. Some of their neighbours were scandalised, not that they were 'a pair of lezzers', but because they had posh home-counties accents.

The three girls went to the Nightjar, which was the only pub in the vicinity. It crouched at the bottom of the rise, a brick-built bunker covered in pigeon scat with the flats sprawling over the top, connected by stairwells and loosely organised into a series of 'walks' named after scientists who had been Ada Lovelace's cronies and contemporaries: Babbage, Dalton, Rutherford, Faraday, Garnett.

'A very forward-thinking woman, Ada Lovelace,' said Louisa.

'Quite the inspiration,' said Harpo.

Petra wouldn't have disagreed, but neither did she want to admit that she was actually more thrilled by Ada's pedigree as Byron's daughter than by her feminist credentials as a mathematician and a proto-computer geek.

The Nightjar was one of those pubs where every head turns to clock newcomers and was not for the faint-hearted. Inside, it was utilitarian with lino floors and an impressive array of electronic machines, cigarette vending, jukebox, one-arm bandits, arcade games – slots all clamouring for coin. Petra ordered three crème de menthe frappés, which was their latest thing. Kenneth, the barman, was astounded.

'Blimey!' he said. 'We've not sold any of that since the year ABBA won the Eurovision Song Contest.' The cap was completely sugared solid, and he had to run it under the hot tap to get it loose.

They picked a table. There were plenty to choose from.

'Your flatmates seem nice, for blokes, I mean,' said Louisa.

'Yeah, well, I should be out quite a lot. But not here, obviously.' Petra gazed around the bar at the early-doors clientele, judging them as saddos slumped in corners nursing bitter, and losers leaning on machines, lost in space.

Harpo didn't bother with conversation; she just scowled at the two skinheads decked out in identical T-shirts and turned up jeans. They were playing pool and kept glancing over as if fancying their chances. In those days, you could still smoke in the pub, and she chain-smoked prison-thin rollies, sitting with one boot up on the other knee, striking matches on her sole.

About seven o'clock, the girls left the pub. The two skins were outside, sitting on the wall, seeing who could spit the furthest. Petra didn't notice them till one called out.

'Yo! Any of you girls up for a bit of cock?'

She turned and smiled pleasantly. Louisa kept walking, kept linking Harpo. Harpo stopped, shook her arm free and retraced her steps.

'What did you say?'

'Oh no! Not the ugly one!' They cracked up, cackling with laughter and slapping each other on the back. Harpo stood square in front of them.

'Come on then, you pair of fuckwits,' she said, *sotto voce*. 'You think you're hard? You think you're hard men? You know what I think? I think you got no balls.'

'Piss off, you fat ugly cow.'

'Soft-arses, the pair of you.'

'Who you calling soft, you 'orrible dyke?'

'Yeah, dyke.'

'Wankers.'

'Fat dyke.'

'Jelly babies.'

'Fat ugly dyke.'

'Fuck nuggets.'

'Dyke.'

'Goatsuckers.'

They traded insults for a while, then Simon, the one with the scar from being born with a hare lip, he got mad and threw a punch, and Gareth, the other one, put in the fourteen-hole AirWair boot. Louisa clung to an astonished Petra; it was over in seconds. Harpo took the kicking and wiped a little blood from her mouth with the back of her hand. She winked at the boys and walked away.

'Is she whistling?' asked Gareth. They listened.

'Hitler – has only got – one – ball,' said Simon.

~

Back at Number 40 Faraday Walk, Stan and Woody discussed changing the lock on the glazed door that led out onto their balcony, but they couldn't see how anyone might get in that way.

FEBRUARY 1982

The Big Stink

They say there is no community spirit in Lovelace Flats. They are wrong. If one of the neighbours is in difficulties, you can rely on everyone coming out to see what's going on. They say there's no love. Love thy neighbour. No choice. We don't choose our neighbours. But we keep an eye out for one another. An eye for an eye.

One morning, Sycorax couldn't sleep, she usually slept until at least midday, but an insidious thin yellow light had crept in and roused her. She pulled on a pair of stockings, straining to get them up her thighs, thick socks, a pair of wellington boots, and with a coat flung over her nightie, she went down to Khalil's shop for milk and Pop-Tarts. While he served her, Mr Khalil was careful to maintain eye contact with his cash register. Everyone said she was a witch. He wasn't sure if it was true, he wasn't sure if he believed in witches, but all the same, he was afraid of her; perhaps we all were. She knew this, and she skewered Mr Khalil with her dark narrow eyes, as if she saw right into him, as if she reached into his head and snatched his thoughts, picked them over, sucked the bones of them and tossed them back.

On impulse and to serve him right for not looking, she slipped a jar of chilli powder into the pocket of her fun-fur coat. There was pork in her fridge, been there since last week, flimsy white plastic wrapping oozing now, sell-by long gone. She hated things going to waste; things paid for by renting out her hole to men who grafted, or men on benefits, or the men who begged, borrowed, and stole. Men who spent their money with her despite their fear – or perhaps because of it? Anyway, they were all passing coin, hand to hand, hand to mouth. Counting it out, wages of sin. Coin circulating – and pork costs coin. Don't waste it. Spice it up, girl!

Coming back from the shop, Sycorax saw a crowd was gathering at the far end of her walkway and went to see what was happening. Of course she did. Some were standing like monuments with their arms folded. They were the old guard, diaspora of the city, a muttering chorus in proper wool coats, indestructible bomb-proof coats that would most likely outlive their occupants. Those old ones, they lived here before, before the slum clearances, living in back-to-backs or caves, and after they were cleared out, they seeped back in. And they were eternally pessimistic; they never missed an opportunity to be disgruntled or to declare that we're all going to hell in a handcart.

Others, incomers, and colonists in anoraks and nylon bombers, with no axe to grind and nothing better to do, indeed, nothing else to do at all, they were leaning on the railings, bumming fags, and exchanging pleasantries. And the lah-di-dah students that had moved in next door to Sycorax, they were there too: him, the tall one, in sports kit and bruised brawny legs, her shivering in a tie-dye frock and twirling her hair. Not the pretty boy that plays the horn, though, no sign of him.

Two blokes from the council in high viz were there, and the police, two of them too, and hefty. Always in twos, they didn't ever come here alone.

'Stand back!'

To a man, the crowd leaned forward. The coppers swung the big red doorknocker and broke down the door of Number 81, and as the timber splintered and capitulated, a collective cry went up from the crowd.

'Aughhh!'

Now they were standing back.

They were miming a big stink. Hands to their noses and mouths, gagging. Gurning theatrically, hands wafting, turning away in disgust. The police, shielding their noses and mouths with blue bent serge arms, stepped up and went in. The crowd craned forward. Sycorax sniffed the air and listened to the speculation:

'That's Mr Kite's, eighty-one.'

'What, him as wears two pairs of trousers?'

'That's him.'

'Anyone seen him about lately?'

'Bad-tempered bastard he is.'

'*Was* most like.'

'No?'

'Been done in, I expect.'

Sycorax heard a wail of sirens coming up the Wells Road, but the tone changed; it went speeding past. Some other drama, not this one.

'How's your Brenda?

'Just the same, duck.'

'Shhh, they're coming out.'

The police emerged, grim-faced. One stood in the doorway, snorting down his nose. One stepped away, speaking into his squawky-talky. From those closest, the info spread like a stain.

'Brown bread he is.'

'Been lying there for days.'

'More than half-cooked – he was on the floor.'

‘On the kitchen floor, see?’

‘With that underfloor heating.’

‘No?’

‘Like hog roast.’

If it had been summer, there would have been flies for sure, Sycorax thought. Colonies of bluebottles thriving and multiplying in the ooze of old Mr Kite. But it was February, still fucking freezing, insects in hibernation, and everyone had the heating on full blast. Because the heating was all-in with the rent, nobody turned it down. If things get too hot, just open a window, let the heat out, heat the whole of the East Midlands if you like.

An hour later, Sycorax saw a private ambulance arrive with a black zip bag and a trolley that folded like scissors. They carried the trolley up the stairwells and pushed it on squeaky wheels along the walkways to collect the partially cooked remains. The smell lingered.

South Georgia, February 1982

Dearest Mama,

Thank you for the coffee. Sometimes I open the tin, just a fraction, to smell the beans and think of you and Mrs Fernandez sitting out on the veranda eating those little sugar cakes.

Your Georg

Being Skint and What to Do About It

Petra was skint. She had spent her student grant, all of it. Now she was taking the moral high ground by taking no more hand-outs from her mother who was, in turn, subsidised by 'that vile pervert', her stepfather.

'How come you've always got money, Stan?' she asked.

'Dunno. Not out on the razz midweek, and don't shop at Chelsea Girl and Miss Selfridge, I suppose.'

Stanley was frugal, except when it came to oil paints. He supplemented his grant with some sports coaching at a posh grammar school so he could afford a ritual Saturday post-match piss-up and curry with the lads of the first XI.

'Yeah, that's got to stop – the shopping, I mean,' she said.

'You could always ask Rockefeller for a sub.' Stan inclined his head towards Mr Rockefeller's room, where the staccato stutter of a typewriter mimicked rapid rifles as Woody worked on that week's magnum opus. Woody was the only child of aged and doting parents who kept him in Sobranie cigarettes and endless jazz sessions at the Black Boy.

'Naah. Awkward.'

'Have you thought about going on the game?'

'Nooo,' she shuddered. 'But I've got an interview for a job at a wine bar.'

'Same thing, girl. Same thing.'

Stan took the lid off the tea caddy and put in three fivers – his share of the rent.

~

Up and down the five walks of Lovelace Flats, pennies are pinched, empty pockets flap, groceries are on tick, pints on the slate, everything else on the never-never. Pawn tickets are tucked in safe places, television sets are repossessed, small-claims court defendants are summonsed, loan sharks circle, gamblers lose. Accounts are overdrawn, credit facilities withdrawn. Stuff gets pinched. Scroungers scrounge, and scrimpers scrape. Lead is swung, benefits claimed, workers do hobbles. Cups of sugar are borrowed, bellies ache, things are eked out. Ends that don't meet are *made* to meet. Ciggies are bummed, gear is shifted. Cash is king, brother. Cash is king.

Space Cadet

Space Invaders. Start. Player 1. Down come the invaders: five rows, eleven aliens in each row, down and down and down, whining, droning like doodlebugs. And underneath, the insistent bass thrub, relentless pulse, heartbeat of a slumbering space monster. Player 1, the hero, slides his shooter from bunker to bunker – a row of little detached houses. Those alien invaders, they keep coming, and they keep firing. Their fire squirts down, straight and vertical like stair rods, and the hero's little-house hiding places crumble away, decimated, desiccated, rubble, dust, nothing, and defeat is inevitable. No surrender, no armistice or amnesty, fight to the death. Game Over. No Credit.

Callum McCandless from 39 Faraday Walk, played, money permitting, all day, every day in the bar of the Nightjar. Kenneth would find him waiting outside when he opened up. Sometimes, Callum was still there at shut tap.

'Last orders, ladies and gentlemen. Last orders,' Kenneth would shout.

And at the end of drinking-up time: 'Come on now, let's be having you. Haven't you got homes to go to?'

Then our space cadet would reluctantly leave his post and return to Sycorax, his motherwitch.

Callum battled against the alien invasion every day; played on till his money ran out. Then he found he could earn extra, out the back – or in the toilets if it was raining. He had a baby face, broad as a bean with thin blonde hair, and the old fellers would tap him up, offer him a quid. At first, he felt awkward, kneeling, but it was easy money.

An Eyewitness Account of What Happened to That Hateful Bastard, Rex Villiers, and What Happened Afterwards

Because the flat was unoccupied, with mounting rent arrears, the tenancy agreement relating to 40 Faraday Walk had been terminated by the City Council in December 1981, and that flat, plus four others, earmarked for a controversial pilot scheme.

Last year, the papers said: VICIOUS ATTACK – LOCAL BUSINESSMAN VICTIM OF HIT-AND-RUN.* As if Rex Villiers was a victim. At Lovelace Flats, we would tell it different. We'd say he deserved everything he got. Deserved to be blasted to smithereens, blasted to a flatness by a borrowed van that ran him over and over and over. Ran him over in forward and then reverse gear till he was pancaked. All his bones disconnected from the thigh bone, and the knee bone, and chicken wing, Kentucky sizzlers. All his ribs were spare and bite-sized, his muscles minced, and his organs pulped to burger relish and spread up the kerb. He had it coming.

Villiers was a predator, drug-pusher, pimp, a complete bastard bully who'd run things around here for too long. He was dipping in everyone's pocket, and one way or another, we were all getting taxed or shafted. For days afterwards, people went to the spot where Villiers got spread, just to spit on it. One poor fucked-up little skank said she found his spleen in the gutter, and she fed it to her dog.

*'VICIOUS ATTACK – LOCAL BUSINESSMAN VICTIM OF HIT-AND-RUN', *East Midlands Gazette*, 22 October 1981.

The papers said the bastard Villiers was mown down. Well, that one man who went to mow (and we all knew who he was), he was hailed as a hero. Before it all happened, mind you, people said he was headshot. Dave Keane used to live alone on Faraday Walk, next door to Sycorax. He was ex-military, freaky, running man, running all over the woods with a rucksack full of bricks on his back. Mumbling to himself and counting things. Tattoos of words all up his arms. Freaky private, control freak. People stepped out of his way, because of him being ex-military and because of him being headshot. But after, well then, he was accorded hero status. Dave Keane was a guardian angel, an avenging spirit. A true vigilante.

The police investigated. They went round door-to-door asking everyone. *Of course*, no one had seen anything. No one said anything. They put posters up asking for information. No one said anything. They offered a reward for information. Then someone said.

When they came to make the arrest, we all heard the sirens come wailing up the Wells Road, and there was plenty who made it their business to be out of their doors and on the walks to watch. The police, anticipating bother, parked the squad cars and two riot vans down at the bottom and came running up in helmets and stab vests. Keane put up a good fight, and the neighbours were cheering him on, hoping he'd break free, make a run for it up to the woods, away on his toes. But he never. Anyway, it took eight of them to hold him down, get him in handcuffs. Fold him in two like a pipe cleaner, push him in the squad car, 'mind yer 'ed, son'.

Later, there was a rumour that it was Sycorax's boy, that poor dumb-fuck Callum, who grassed. They got that wrong. He wasn't the one who could see where this might go. He wasn't the one who could see that Keane had to be stopped because he *was* headshot. Keane heard voices in between his ears, and heaven knows who those voices might whisper about. Who might be next on his hit list?

Getting Real

Petra got offered the part-time job at the fancy wine bar down in the city.

'Heels? Really?'

'Yep,' said Celeste. 'If you want the job. High heels make your legs look better, longer. And a lot of our punters are leg men.'

'That's so sexist!'

'You want tips? You wear heels. That's economics.'

Celeste worked there full time, low pay, long hours. She was from the city, born and bred with an accent as broad as the Trent. Sometimes, after work, Celeste and Petra went for a drink.

'So, these two blokes you live with, is one of them your feller then?'

'No, just mates.'

'Straight up? No hanky-panky?'

'No way! Not my type, not either of them.' Under the table, Petra crossed her fingers in case she had told a lie.

'Good girl. You gotta hold out for someone special. Someone with class. And assets.' Celeste fluffed up her candyfloss hair for the benefit of two city gents, suited and booted, and looking their way. Petra mimed her evaluation and disgust. Celeste laughed, warm and throaty like treacle.

'You're worse than my kid sister,' she said. 'She's got her head up her arse too. You need to wise up.'

‘They’re a bit stiff,’ said Petra. ‘And a bit old.’

‘Old enough to treat you right, not like the dickhead college boys you hang about with. All them spotty brainboxes with tiny grants, and lah-di-dah poshos sponging off of mater and pater, or them arty types living on lentils.’

‘But–’

‘The trouble with you is, you’re wet behind the ears, duck.’

‘But–’

But Celeste was *real*. Petra found that with her, she could relax and stop pretending to like modern jazz, concept art, and Brechtian theatre. Stop pretending she understood the difference between existentialism and nihilism. She could stop trying to seem intellectual, which she found exhausting. She spent less and less time with Louisa (ballet pumps), Harpo (jackboots), and the well-heeled, well-read, creative underachievers who drifted around campus, and she spent more time in the city. Sure, the wine bar had its cynics and charlatans, but it was a world away from the supercilious disengagement of the polytechnic art department, so brittle, witty and insincere. Their hearts on ice, and unblinking lizard eyes everywhere, seeing nothing.

‘They come here and see nothing,’ said Celeste. ‘I think lizards have an extra eyelid for blanking out the sun. Maybe students have an extra eyelid for blanking out what’s real.’

‘Maybe there are different types of real,’ said Petra, stretching for some middle ground.

‘No, duck. Real is real. And zip your bag up – anyone could dip their hand in that. You gotta start looking out for yourself, especially up at Lawless Flats. My Aunty June used to live up there. The council put her there after they knocked down Albemarle Street. It was the first time she’d ever had an inside toilet, but that didn’t compensate. Anyway, she went mad as a badger. It was like the old Wild West up there at the flats. Do they still light bonfires on the rooftops?'

'I've never seen anything like that,' said Petra.

'And throw all the rubbish out of the windows?'

'Well, yeah, that.'

'And there was a witch. Honest to God. A *bona fide* witch. They said she could turn people into toads.'

'Yeah?'

'But I hear the flats have gone proper rough these days with drugs and gangs. Not safe to go out on your own. They make snuff films up there, you know? You wanna be extra careful going home on your own after work.'

'It doesn't seem so bad,' said Petra. 'I just wish it wasn't so far away from everything. That bus up the Wells Road takes an eternity.'

'Well, you take care, duck, the things that go on. Did you get one of them pepper sprays like I told you?'

'I think they are illegal.'

'Yeah. So is rape.'

MARCH 1982

South Georgia, March 1982

Constantino Davidoff and a gang of forty-one scrap metal workers return to South Georgia to begin dismantling the old whaling stations. Again, the paperwork is not quite in order. Some saw it as provocation. The British newspapers were full of it.

Dearest Mama,

I am back in hell. I know now that hell is not a place of fires but of ice and wind. The crossing from the mainland was made in very bad weather, and I think we will be stuck here for many weeks. The workers, forty big men who brag that they are hard men, hard as nails, were overcome with relief when we landed. Some lay face down on the shore, some making prayers. Then they got their *cojones* back and celebrated with liquor and song and hoisting the flag; *la bandera azul y blanca* flies over South Georgia again.

Now they whine about the cold, and the sleeping huts, and the wind. How it howls through the old oil tanks, how the ventilation shafts clatter and bang. They say the place is haunted. They say the food is shit and try to shoot reindeer for fresh meat.

I crack the whip. I tell them they must work faster, work better, put backs into it, then we can all go home to our families. Constantino is still fucking asshole, he stays mostly in the radio shack where he makes his office, smoking.

Georg

P.S. Out in the bay, we catch glimpses of a British ship of immense size.* It patrols like a killer whale, and I fear it is an evil sign. Constantino laughs. He says it will turn tail any day now.

---

*HMS *Endurance* (3,658 tons) Royal Navy Ice Patrol Vessel. In 1982, the bright red ship, nicknamed *The Red Plum*, was supporting the British Antarctic Survey. Shuttling between the Falklands and South Georgia, it was so often in the right place at the wrong time.

Dancing Queens

Celeste took Petra dancing, and Petra went home with a scaffolder called Adam.

'Two mistakes in one night. Not too clever,' Stan said later.

But Petra liked Celeste. She was 'from' the city, always lived there, her patch. She had big hair, wore neon tights and drank white wine spritzers. She was into Duran Duran but had never seen *Barbarella*. Celeste was real, and her pleasures were real. Petra's old friends from the polytechnic, the 'lentil-eating, arty types', could only enjoy things metaphorically or at arm's length. They only danced as Nietzsche would. Soooo ironic.

They agreed to meet at a bar down in the city. Petra arrived first and was amused to see how Celeste shuddered, picking her way through a throng of shit-faced DipEds doing tequila slammers. They were braying like asses, the chosen ones, inheritors of the earth, and Celeste moved among them as if they were radioactive, holding her bag close, avoiding contamination. Then she took one look at Petra and steered her to the ladies to fix her make-up. Petra tried to explain about Jane Fonda and the orgasmatron, but Celeste said shut up while she did lip liner.

'Kiss,' she ordered, holding out a piece of toilet paper to blot.

'Drink?' Petra asked.

'Not here, duck,' she said, recoiling like Petra had suggested they drink straight out of the toilet bowl. 'Come on, I know a place.'

Arm in arm, they sashayed through the sodium glare of the night city.

~

Celeste took Petra to a club, the sort none of Petra's student friends would ever go to. It was off the main drag – you'd never stumble across it by accident – down a warren of backstreets, up a fire escape. Celeste knew the doormen. Of course, she did. And they were built like brick shithouses, as all doormen should be. Probably lived on a diet of protein milkshakes and sixteen-egg omelettes.

'Gary B and Gaz the spaz – don't call him that to his face,' Celeste hissed.

'Alright, Celeste. Long time,' said Gary B, drinking her in. 'Is she cool, your mate?'

'Yeah, course. But she's new, so give her the spiel.'

He hesitated. 'Student?'

'Noooo. Works with me at the wine bar.'

Gary nodded, reassured that Petra wasn't one of the undesirable subspecies. He stamped the backs of their hands, handed each of them a paper plate and waved towards a trestle table with peanuts, chicken drumsticks, and bowls of rice salad.

'Due to certain unfavourable conditions on our liquor licence, we are serving a buffet supper. If the law comes, and the music stops, you make sure you got food on your plate.' He grinned, showing gold-capped teeth. '*Comprendez*?'

Celeste winked and patted his arm. As they went in, Petra glanced back and saw Gaz the spaz gazing after Celeste, like that cartoon bulldog with eyes like saucers.

~

It's early; the room barely quarter full, a mobile disco pumping out obscure dance tracks full throttle. They go to the bar, spritzer for Celeste, cider for Petra. Steadily the place fills. Working people, strutting in, greeting, jostling. Friday night. After forty or fifty hours serving, stamping, checking, fixing, cutting, typing, shovelling, pressing-the-button, and screw-ing-the-bobbin, they have clocked off and dressed up. They are all out to spend brass, on the razz, here to dance, make a night of it, an all-nighter. Pools of light form and dissolve, strobe and ultraviolet. The beat is relentless; can you feel it? So loud, non-stop, pulsing, lip-read, feel-the-force, feels like heaven, spinning, spinning, feet on fire, feel no pain, dance the night away, dance, and devil-may-care, dance like no one is watching, and dance yourself dizzy.

Petra finds herself wrapped in the absolute thisness of the moment. Dazzled by the light now emanating from her own skin, she knows she is a perfect star in a perfect galaxy. Now she is part of the city; she fits, she's a player, she's connected, she radiates, she is real. By midnight, Petra and Celeste are both knocking back room-temperature Blue Nun, and the place is heaving and sweaty with dancing queens.

Rice salad glistens under the spinning lights.

Asteroids

Asteroid (noun). Rocky, airless little world incapable of supporting life. Trajectory: orbital or co-orbital. Composition: rock or mineral. Surface: volatile. Earth collision: inevitable, possibly imminent.

At the Nightjar, the Space Invader machine still lurks by the passageway to the gents. But then Kenneth goes all modern and gets Asteroids, vector graphics, deceptively simple, compellingly addictive. At first, Callum plays both games, then mostly Asteroids, then just Asteroids. Now, he plays Asteroids all day, existing only to play Asteroids, feeling no hunger for anything except the white rocks that come at him, and he blasts them to pieces, to smithereens small enough to swallow them down, and he feels nothing, as if he doesn't quite exist.

He's skying through the void, thrusting into hyperspace. He is flying, aiming, pivoting, blasting, weightless in space, a space junky, fighter pilot, galactic superstar, a hero. HERO. He pivots and blasts. The rocks get smaller and faster, smaller faster, smallerfaster. Then the game ends, his credit is gone, he needs to stretch his cramped muscles and to suck the cock of the mithering old fucker waiting, eyeing, rubbing, fumbling in his trouser pocket for a couple of quid.

When Callum shuts his eyes, he finds he can still see white rocks, like planet rock cake, coming at him out of the blackness of infinity. They zoom towards the vanishing point at the back of his eyes, or maybe at the back of his throat, and they come, and they come, and they come. ZOOM! And he vanishes into a point of light at the apex of the blaster. A star exploding into a supernova, imploding into a black hole that swallows him, swallows the Nightjar, swallows Lovelace Flats and the City and England and Europe and Planet Earth and the Galaxy and the Universe and Everything.

~

His mother doesn't care how Callum earns his money or what he spends it on. She smooths the lank hair back from his pale forehead, though he flinches at her touch. Maybe even *she* needs someone to love. Maybe. She curses the ones she hates, and they disappear up her snatch. But not her boy. He came out that way. He won't go back. She's amused that he hates her; he was never the full shilling, she thinks.

But Sycorax senses trouble. She sees that he's got into the habit of screwing his eyes tight shut, playing Asteroids in his head. He doesn't see what he has coming.

Nine Lives

Four: Crouched behind a tower of old plastic milk crates, he was still to the point of invisibility. Watching, waiting for the vermin that could be supper. Mr Khalil was busy stacking tins of cat food on his shelves in the shop, but they were for paying customers, not for work-shy fleabags who must pull own bloody weight and earn own bloody keep; take responsibility for bloody pest control.

He sniffs. Fine whiskers quiver either side of his curiously unbeautiful face, his inner eyelid darts and retracts. The tip of his tail is alert, a metronome. Come on, come on. In the corner, by the blocked drainpipe where it's dry, brown dirt, brown leaves, multicoloured litter, silver and blue, becoming faded and forgotten, then, at last, a little brown scurrying. Pounce.

Three: Home was the stuffy and overfurnished flat above the Nightjar. He was a young house cat full of braggadocio and not allowed out. He sharpened his claws on the chintzy three-piece just to pass the time, and he shat in a tray of grit, or next to it.

He was the plaything of two girls – the spoiltbrat daughters of Kenneth's then-wife. They named him Bluebell-Pinklepur, dressed him up in frocks and bonnets, pushed him about in the doll's pram, and fought over which of them loved him the very most. But one day, sick of bonnets and screaming girl-fights, Pinklepur put out his claws and scrammed one of them across the face. Her mouth was a perfect O, then the noise started.

'This is all your fault, Ken,' the then-wife shrieked. 'I said this would happen. I said it, didn't I? Look at the state of her. Get an ambulance.'

'It's a scratch.'

'She's bleeding, Ken. It'll get infected. They're full of disease, filthy animals. Look at the way it retches up them disgusting furballs. It could have rabies.'

'That's dogs, my precious. Just put some TCP on it.'

'Fucking TCP? Are you mad? She might be scarred for life. She might need plastic surgery.'

After the row that ensued, the then-wife and her daughters moved out. Kenneth hitched up his drooping kecks and took to the bottle. Ten green bottles, sometimes more. Because of the drinking, he often forgot to feed the bloody cat, and one day, he forgot to shut the bloody door.

Two: He was in an enormous glass tankworld with sawdust in his fur and people walking past. If he bothered to look, he saw mostly their legs and shoes and shopping bags. With his unattractive mottlecoat of dusty black and stained white, he was the last to be picked. Sometimes children banged on the glass to see him startle and hiss, or they pressed their faces right up against it, wheedling.

'Pleeeeeese.'

'Whining, pouting little minxes. Nothing but trouble from arsehole to breakfast time,' said Kenneth under his breath, but he gave in and got them a kitten, so they could be a proper family, so that he might keep his new, sour-faced, then-wife sweet.

One: Before that, there was milk and there was sleeping. Gradually his eyes opened, blue at first, then becoming yellowish. He learned to fight his siblings for a place on the dug. *There* was bliss. Lying between the others, all perpendicular to the flank of the mothercat, kneading with their little, pink-padded paws and their velcro claws until their bellies swelled tight as tics. Then there was being licked and cuffed. He learned to pounce.

Five: On impulse, Mrs Sharpe from Dalton Walk reached down and scooped up the fleabag; she was sorely in need of something to love. Mr Khalil raised his colossal eyebrows but didn't protest. After all, he was used to people helping themselves. Mrs Sharpe took the cat home and called him Betsy after a cat in a storybook she remembered from when she was a child. He didn't mind. He got regular meals, fattened up a bit, slept on a knitted blanket in a cardboard box. It reminded him of the mothercat.

Then *Mr* Sharpe was released on parole. He came home with a curfew and a hard-on. He kicked the cardboard box and stated right away that next, he would 'kick the cat to kingdom come'.

Six: To save the cat from a good ribroasting, Mrs Sharpe took it to her husband's uncle on Garnett Walk. He apologised for answering the door in his vest. He was doing the ironing.

'What do I want with a frigging cat?'

'Go on, Ralph, it'd do you good to have some company.'

Ralph liked the company of young lads, not cats, but he took it, perhaps because of the fresh bruises on her face.

'Well, I can't call it Betsy – have you seen the knackers on it?'

'No.'

'It's a tomcat, alright. People round here will think I'm some frigging weirdo if he has a girl's name. They'll call me a poofter. I can't have that, duck.'

The cat became Mungo and developed a taste for tinned fish – sardines, mackerel, anchovies. Ralph used to be in the Merchant Navy, and now, marooned inland, he liked to feast on the fruits of the ocean. But Ralph began to wheeze a great deal and eventually, regretfully, conceded that he was allergic to his new shipmate.

Seven: Mungo went to live with miserable old Mr Kite on Faraday Walk. Mr Kite had a cat flap in the balcony door so Mungo could come and go as he pleased. The two of them lived there for years. Mr Kite shoplifted tins of Kit-e-kat, and Mr Khalil turned a blind eye. Sometimes Mr Kite would piss the bed and blame the cat, but he never punished him or shut him out.

Eight: After Mr Kite became a neglected corpse and the police forced entry, and the stink was something terrible, the cat continued to live at 81 Faraday Walk, and he continued to come and go as he pleased, now feeding on foraged remains of takeaways and roadkill. Then men from the council came with chipboard to seal up the doors and windows.

'Bugger me! It don't half hum in here,' said one of them.

'Feral cat, I suppose.'

Nine: Mungo was forced to relocate. He'd have preferred a home without children.

Hold Your Tongue

Friday night. Stan is soaking paint brushes in jars of turps. Despite the windows being wide open, the kitchen stinks. Woody is already out – he's down in the city at the Black Boy, with a ticket to see ace jazz saxophonist, Evan Parker. Petra has a date with a bloke who chatted her up at the wine bar. She pretends she's meeting friends in the student union, but Stan clocks that she's too dressed up for that.

'Come on then, Slap, who is he?'

He is nearly thirty and drives an Opel Manta. Petra cannot divulge these things for fear of ridicule. Stan gave her a hard enough time over the scaffolder. The bus into the city is due in eight minutes. She storms out.

She prances down the concrete stairwell and across the concrete amphitheatre. Radiation Man is there in a new tinfoil hat and a pair of sunglasses with only one lens. He's examining a suitcase that isn't his. He waves at her in semaphore. Petra trots on. The bus is due in five minutes.

Outside the Nightjar, a ruckus.

'No, it wasn't me. I never. He was my friend.'

'You haven't got any friends.'

'Mr Keane wouldn't have a rat-faced cocksucker like you for a friend.'

'He was. Ask anyone.'

'What? Ask your mother?'

'Shut the fuck up, you faggot.'

'I never said nothing.'

'This'll learn you.'

'Yeah. To hold your tongue.'

'Kick him, Si.'

'I never grassed him up. I never. Aarrgh.'

'Faggot.'

'Snitch.'

'Oh! Help. Geroff. No. Stop.'

'Keep yer mouth shut, faggot.'

In the light spilling from the pub windows, Petra sees three figures. The two boys that dress like twins, always at the pool table, leering a little, lording it, and a shapeless lump crouched on the ground with his hands over his head: a giant toad in a beige anorak with stuffing coming loose. The boys are kicking the toad. They are booted and angular-long-limbed like stick-men, heads shaved close as bullets, one with a funny lip. They used to run errands for some bloke called Rex Villiers, but he's dead, and now they don't have to. Now they have another hero, now they avenge him. They are no angels. Listen closely, you might hear the *crack* as Callum's jawbone shatters.

Petra checks her little clutch bag for change. The bus is due in three minutes.

Pentimento: Stanley Harbours a Grudge

Pentimento (noun) From the Italian pentirsi, *to repent. A term used in art to describe the revealed or residual image of a previous version that haunts a painting. Evidence of something the painter has changed his mind about or struggled to get right.*

Stan was staring out of the kitchen window and sketching. Colossal concrete battlements casting shade, lines of power cables strung from pylons, the earthworks of the bypass. He was working on a series of sketches for a new oil painting of monolith slabs, megalith strata, the rise of the land that draws the eye, a perfect golden sector beneath a thin and empty sky. The canvas was vast; stretched, primed, and ready. Too vast to transport on the number 42 bus. Stan peered down to the ground below. A thin black dog was rummaging through the litter that accumulated like high-water flotsam around the flats. The dog sniffed and pissed, sniffed and pissed. Stan was fascinated by the shape of the dog as it made a tripod of itself, and its spine twisted in contrapposto.

Petra flounced in dressed something like a cross between Tinkerbelle and Captain Hook. She sprawled at the table, sighed theatrically, got out her sketch pad and fiddled with some charcoal. She started drawing Woody, who was lounging against the kitchen counter, completely absorbed in reading *The Balcony* by Jean Genet and occasionally stirring his lentil dahl concoction.

Stan's eyes flicked inside, outside. Distraction. His concentration fractured.

'Stick the kettle on then, Slap.'

'Busy. Do it yourself.' She emitted a noise that indicated artistic temperament and the frustration of a perfectionist. She ripped out the top page of the pricey A3 Bockingford cold-pressed, scrunched it to a ball, and tossed it on the kitchen floor.

'I'll have an Earl Grey if you're offering,' said Woody without taking his eyes off the Genet.

Petra filled the kettle and flicked the switch.

Not the brightest. Petra. Fawning over Woody, making him cups of fancy tea, Assam, Darjeeling darling. Woody played along sometimes, sometimes not. Sometimes he drank the tea, sometimes not. Stanley had bog-standard brown tea, milk and two sugars. Woody should man up. She sketched him, Woody that is, pensive, glowering, dreaming, lost. Blind to Petra's adoration-bordering-on-infatuation. She had charcoal all over her fingers, a smudge by her mouth. She had him in profile, hawkish nose, an air of indifference; it wasn't bad. Not bad for her anyway. But she fidgeted, incapable of looking properly, incapable of concentration, uncomfortable with the silence.

'Would you rather be... deaf or blind?' she said at last.

'If you pick deaf, perhaps you could be dumb as well, please?' said Woody, eyes still on Genet.

'Naughty! But like the song says, "I would rather go blind". And you?'

Woody relented. 'Yeah, okay, I'd rather be blind. Then I wouldn't have to see this godforsaken, ugly, shithole of a place.'

'Well, I'd much rather be deaf,' said Stan, even though he really hadn't intended to say anything at all. 'Yeah, I'd pick deaf. Especially if Woody was practicing his bloody horn.'

'You gotta practice, man,' Woody drawled.

'But it sounds like utter shite.'

'Sounds to me like you've got a tin ear.'

Stan and Woody glared at one another as if the game counted for something.

'Okay, boys. Easy. What would you rather eat, cat or dog?'

'Oh, cat. Definitely cat,' said Woody. 'Can we eat the one that keeps shitting on our balcony?'

Ooh! That's horrid,' said Petra.

'Well, you asked.'

'Will you two shut the fuck up?'

Maybe they were both already blind. Stan gazed out of the window seeing only the most indescribable beauty. They were both so vain but understood nothing of real beauty – the beauty of things, solid things. Petra, the butterfly, Woody, the spider. For Petra, Lovelace was the back of beyond, and more and more, she stayed away. At first, she stayed with friends from the polytechnic, down at the campus, but increasingly, she spent her time with Celeste. Bloody Celeste. Woody too seemed unsettled. He said that Lovelace was his purgatory, a threshold, a liminal place. He carped on about 'bad vibes' and 'dark atmospheres' and about the smell. How he needed his space, man. Needed a rocket up his arse, more like.

Stanley had come to see Lovelace as the most beautiful place he had ever lived. The landscape, the scars of civilization scrawled across the terrain like graffiti. He saw it as blocks of colour, planes and facets, changing with the light. The concrete was a thousand, thousand shades: alabaster, anthracite, graphite, mauve, moss, quartz, rust, sable, zircon. He saw shade, line, chiaroscuro, dapple, pentimento. Schematically, Lovelace was a labyrinth. It was a maze, jigsaw, perfect tangram. And beyond everything, the tangled, brooding mass of the forest, hunkered down and ancient. Even in sunlight, the forest was a green much darker than black. Stan struggled to put it into words, but he saw it. The kitchen window was his panopticon. He was the eye.

He painted obsessively, mixed paint in his dreams. It was ingrained in his skin; he smelt of oils and turpentine. All he wanted for the rest of his life was to live *there* and to paint what he saw. And for them to shut the fuck up.

APRIL 1982

The War on Circulation: Kelvin MacKenzie Gains Another Reader

From the off, The Sun *adopted a gung-ho attitude to the Falklands War, revelling in gallows humour and jingoistic rabble-rousing.* The Sun *never passed up an opportunity to support 'Our Boys', poke fun at 'The Argies', or to shame rival newspapers for taking a balanced or – God forbid – a neutral stance to reporting the war. It is editor Kelvin MacKenzie's* Sun *that is remembered for capturing the zeitgeist.*

'Has *The Guardian* not come in yet, Mr Khalil?'

Bloody students. Mr Khalil glares at them from beneath his extraordinary eyebrows and continues rearranging his stock of discount lookalike beefy supernoodles. No, *The Guardian* is not coming. Journalists are on strike, and many newspapers are disrupted. Woody is genuinely dismayed. Stan buys *The Sun* instead. STICK IT UP YOUR JUNTA.* Nice tits.

On their way home, they see Louisa and Harpo heading down to the city. Harpo will buy the *Socialist Worker*. Louisa finds everything she needs in *Tatler*.

*'STICK IT UP YOUR JUNTA', *The Sun*, 20 April 1982.

Buenos Aires, April 1982

On 2 April, Argentine troops arrived in the Falklands/Las Malvinas. After a brief battle, the islands were occupied – or liberated – depending on your viewpoint. The following day, the British base at Grytviken on South Georgia was also occupied/liberated.

Georg, My Darling Boy,

Oh, how I long for you to be home. You should have been here for the celebration. You should have *seen* it. The streets were thronged, it was like a fiesta, everywhere decorated with banners and flags. Blue and white as far as the eye could see. Bands played in the Plaza de Mayo, and the sun shone, it was as if all Argentina marched in joyous celebration of having our own Malvinas back again. Everyone except you, my son, so far from home and playing your small part in our glorious victory.

Mrs Fernandez took many, many photographs of the parades, and you shall see them all when you are home.

Mama

Dearest Georg,

I am worried. No word from you in weeks now. Where are you? The news here is all of Argentine triumph, of course it would be: *ESTAMOS GANANDO!** the papers say, and they

---

*'*ESTAMOS GANANDO!*' (we're winning), *GENTE*, May 1982.

ridicule *La Thatcher*. PIRATA, BRUJA Y ASESINA† they call her. But there are beginning to be unofficial reports of many more English warships and English submarines speeding south.

Mrs Fernandez and I pray for your safe return.

Mama

---

†'*PIRATA, BRUJA Y ASESINA*' (pirate, witch and assassin), *Tal Cual*, 30 April 1982.

Neighbours: In Which Petra Learns What Sycorax Does for a Living

After a long shift at the wine bar, Petra's trotters were like dogmince. She hadn't dared take off her shoes on the bus home for fear they wouldn't go back on again. Now, she eased them off and flicked on the portable TV in the kitchen. The boys were both still out somewhere. Not together. Obviously. She'd barely got comfortable when there was a hesitant tap on the front door. Completely forgetting to put the chain on, she opened it to a taller, cleaner version of Stan. He grinned like a sheep and apologised for the late hour.

'We were supposed to meet at that pub, the one down behind the market, but apparently, I'd missed him, gone for a curry someone said, but I didn't know where, sorry, I had a couple of bevvies on my own, then got a taxi here. The driver wasn't keen, said he'd have to charge me extra.'

'Are you Stan's brother by any chance?'

'Yes, sorry, Neil.' And he fumbled his hand out of his pocket and offered it.

She looked at his hand. It had a piece of used tissue stuck to it.

'He's not back, but come in.'

'You must be Petra?'

She led the way down the still uncarpeted stairs into the kitchen, which she realised without much embarrassment, smelt faintly unpleasant.

'Are you here on your own?' he asked.

'Yeah, just got back from work – my feet are killing.'

'On your own?'

'Yeah.'

'Aren't you scared?'

'Of what?' she scoffed, and Neil blenched.

'I thought I heard you come back, well someone anyway – I hoped it would be Stanley. Your, er, neighbours heard me knocking on your door earlier, and they invited me in.'

'Neighbours?'

With a jerk of his head, Neil indicated Number 39, the door that paired with theirs. Two doors side-by-side, one yellow, one blue, and whilst one set of stairs went up, the other went down. The precise shade of the yellow door, according to Stan, was somewhere between primrose and chronic diarrhoea. After living there for three months, Petra had never actually seen the neighbours; maybe they never went out.

Neil looked slightly traumatized.

'I brought a bottle,' he said. 'Tequila.'

She raised her eyebrows and kicked her shoes into the corner. He didn't seem to have a bottle about him.

'They drank it. Your neighbours, they drank it.'

'All of it?'

'Yup. All of it.'

He sat with his head in his hands. She sniffed the milk and made tea.

'She's huge, that lady, next door. She made me really welcome, but I didn't know where to look. She had on this—' Neil flapped his hands trying to convey a frilled and flounced diaphanous negligée. 'Nightie— and her—' his hands indicated large and pendulous breasts.

Oh, God, it's like charades, thought Petra. I hate charades.

'Then after a bit, there was a man – he came to the door, and the lady took him upstairs, left me with Callum, her son, at least she said he was her son. Pasty looking bloke with blonde hair and a scarred face? No?'

Petra shrugged.

'He just sat staring at me, then he said, "It's only a tenner if you want a go," and I didn't know what he meant.' Neil groaned and ran his hands through his hair. 'Then he came and sat next to me, put his hand on my knee and said, "I'd do you if I could – only a fiver," and I still didn't get what he was saying till he mimed it. I thought that was bad, then he grinned this really lopsided grin with his lips pulled back, and all his teeth were fastened shut with a cat's cradle of silver wire.'

Petra laughed, a brittle made-up laugh because she thought Neil was probably making it up.

'D'you know you're living next to a brothel?' he asked.

The portable television was still on, its screen a porthole to the world – the real world. First, it'd been some palaver about scrap metal workers on South Georgia, then Argentinian soldiers invaded the Falkland Islands. Hardly anyone knew where the Falkland Islands were, but that soon changed because apparently, they were ours. Today, on a quayside somewhere on the south coast, the sun was shining, crowds cheering and waving flags. There was bunting and tears as the young buds of a proud seafaring nation boarded a huge ship bound for the South Atlantic.* In uniforms as white as snow, all starched and pressed, they lined the decks and saluted and

---

*In all, 128 Ships sailed with the Task Force: 43 Royal Navy ships, 22 Royal Fleet Auxiliary ships, 63 merchant ships STUFT (ships taken up from trade) including the cruise ships SS *Canberra*, SS *Uganda*, and the *QEII*.

saluted and saluted as the ship pulled away. The brass bands played. The ship's horns honked farewell, and all the other ships and boats in the harbour honked back like crazy.

Neil's mouth was opening and closing, but Petra had put him on mute while she watched in dismay, the young Billy Budds, pale and smiling, waving from the decks of a destroyer.

Better than Broccoli

Woody had borrowed a video camera for an art installation project he was collaborating on. Before the camera had to go back, he said they'd do a remake of Bond, better than Broccoli. The working title was *The Spy with the Golden Thunderballs*, and he apologised for it being so lightweight:

'...and appallingly middlebrow, and populist, but it might be, er, 'fun'. And we don't have as much 'fun' as I thought we would. I know I've been a bit uptight lately...'

Petra said she hadn't noticed.

Over a lateish breakfast, they cobbled together a script and a running order for the scenes. Then came casting. Petra wanted to be Moneypenny, but the boys said no. She must be Bond, Petra Bond. Woody would be the villain, Scaramanga, and Stan was the love interest with the innuendo name: Kissy Suzuki, Holly Goodhead, Honey Ryder.

'Pussy Galore, wooo-hooo,' he shouted, rummaging, uninvited, through Petra's underwear drawer and selecting a peach-coloured satin balconette bra.

'Oh that,' she said. 'I never wear that. Can't imagine why I bought it.'

Stan strapped it on over his ancient, beloved Che Guevara T-shirt and paraded on the balcony and then along the walkway, pouting. The hyenas gathered, hooting and jeering; Petra vowed never to wear the bra (again). Woody, sporting an eyepatch in order to look villainous, recruited 'extras' from amongst the hyenas: snipers, henchmen, corpses, that sort of thing. At first, the kids were dismissive, ridiculing the film as 'stoopid', but then like dominoes falling, they defected and were queuing up to be involved. Stan's brother Neil would be their cameraman.

Petra felt divided about the film, positively bifurcated. It was as if she could step outside herself and see, from some as yet uninhabited angle, or point in time, that in the pleasure of the thing, there was irony and a double bluff. And an unidentified nagging voice cautioned, 'you're so sharp, Princess, you want to watch you don't cut yourself.' Louisa and Harpo dropped by and pronounced the idea 'such a hoot!' but declined to be involved; they were off to demonstrate against the new bypass. Celeste would have said the whole thing was daft. Celeste would have said, what's the point in making a film that's already been made? Celeste would have put her hands on her hips and declared that they were pretentious arty farts and that cross-dressing really, *really* got her goat. Petra decided it would be best not to mention the film.

~

Towards the end of the afternoon, they were filming 'on location' in Kiev (the bottom of Dalton Walk). A tracking shot. The villain Scaramanga drags Pussy Galore to the nerve centre of his empire of evil, where he will subject her to brutal but imaginative torture as an inducement to make Bond hand over the prototype asteroid deflector gun (water pistol). As Scaramanga and Pussy emerge from the catacombs (the underpass to Khalil's shop), Bond must leap from above and rescue Pussy, who is still wearing the peach satin bra.

Bond, played by Petra in an old tuxedo, was waiting on the grassy bank beside the underpass. With her was a skinny little thing called Ruby who didn't get a part in the film but was the 'assistant to Mr Petra'. Petra tried to show Ruby how to make daisy chains, but the daisies were stunted with insufficient stalk. Ruby watched politely.

It was a sunny cold day. The big pivot windows of the kitchens up above them were wide open, letting out the smell of fried food, the numbing thrub of reggae, free heat, and an occasional empty lager can. St George's flags and Union Jacks flapped from many of the balconies, and somewhere beyond the flags, a woman was shouting: 'I never fucking said that. You know I never.'

Petra studied her assistant. Ruby had bruised thin arms and was just at that age when milk teeth have dropped out, and the big ones started to come through, too big. Adult teeth in a child's mouth. Her dress was also oversized, almost certainly a hand-me-down. It gaped at the front revealing a dirty white vest and sometimes a glimpse of nipple. She had been shy with Petra, but now, waiting for their cue, she talked.

'Will you kill Mr Scaramanga?'

'No, he lives to fight another day.'

'Would you kill him if this were real?'

'Well, if this was real, then no, still no. Killing is wrong.'

'I know a man that got killed. Mr Villiers.'

'That's very sad.'

'Not really. He was a evil bastard. Everybody said.'

'Like Scaramanga?'

'No. Not like a baddie in a film, but like *real*, you know? Like a proper bastard that hurts people. He hurt my sister. Sometimes she still cries about it, but not so much now. Now, she takes medicine. And she's got his spleen in a jar.'

As she spoke, her face took on a narrow, pinched look, and she aged until she was at least a hundred. Petra smiled uncertainly at her – so imaginative. Ruby reached out and took Petra's hand, and Petra made a mental note to have a good bath after this. These kids could have lice or nits or ringworm...

Pussy gave a blood-curdling scream as Scaramanga dragged her past the old burnt-out settee, now a mesh of rusting springs. He dragged her through the underpass, their footsteps ringing, the light menacingly low. Then out they burst, into the heroic brightness beyond. Stan's brother Neil was scooting behind on a borrowed skateboard with the hefty video recorder hoisted onto his shoulder. Petra was looking at the child's nipple.

'Cut!'

'Petra, what the fuck? You missed your cue. Again.'

*Tidespring**

On 25 April, after some initial cockups, problems caused by severe weather conditions, the lucky crippling of Argentine submarine, Santa Fe, *and then a brief skirmish, South Georgia was retaken by British forces. The Argentinian military and the scrap metal men were rounded up and shipped out.*

Down in the steel hull, we sit on what we can. Some play cards for buttons and promises and to pass the time. The rest of us, we sleep, dreaming of promises, and to pass the time. I dream the sides of the tanker are made of glass, and I can see all the thousands of fishes swimming south while we go north. I think we are close now to the equator, which is the world's belly button.

The men have been sick many days and have nothing left to heave up from their guts. Now, less sick, they make more trouble. There is fear, boredom, resentment, blame, bad language, insults, pointless threats. No camaraderie. Davidoff's crew, men used to working away from home, used to working with men – men with calloused hands and nothing to lose – they despise the soldier boys. *Los soldados,* mostly from the north of Argentina with their pale gold skin and soft hands, used to marching in pretty squares, being kissed by girls, and

*RFA *Tidespring* (A75) a 27,400 ton Tide-class replenishment oiler of the Royal Fleet Auxiliary was due to be decommissioned but was reprieved and seconded to the Task Force.

now, with their promised glory snatched, they turn sallow and downcast.

A fight spoils: the two of spades is missing. Accusations fly, and fists are clenched. It cannot be helped, but my money, if I had any, would be on the scrap man. The *Inglés* outside, he bangs on the thick steel door. His meaning is clear enough: 'Shut the fuck up, you bunch of Argy shitheads'. The sound booms through me. My knees are stiff, my beard itches. Probably lice.

Constantino, *Meester* fucking Constantino Davidoff,† he has a cabin, he smokes on deck, and wanders about with hands in pockets. *Bastardo*. I would be glad to be up on deck, feel the wind, instead of crouching here below the waterline. Sailing in the wrong direction, in a fucking sardine tin.

---

†The scrap-metal dealer, Constantino Davidoff (who, after all, had a legitimate contract with British-owned firm Christian Salvesen to dismantle and salvage the four disused whaling stations on South Georgia) will later sue the British government for loss of revenue caused by their interference in his business activities. He will sue them through the Argentinian courts for $200,000,000. And he will be unsuccessful.

Jawbone

Jawbone (noun) Lower mandible, or half of same, submaxilla forming the shape of the face. Jawbone (verb) To persuade or pressurise using superior position, especially to ensure compliance with policy. Masculinity favours a strong bone: Jawbone of an ass.

Word got spread about Lovelace Flats that it was Callum McCandless who had grassed on Dave Keane, our local hero. At first, it was just idle talk and groundless speculation. Then the two boys that used to run errands for Rex Villiers, even though they were not sorry to see the back of him, they took it upon themselves to up the ante. Anyway, Callum said he never. He tried to put them straight, but they said, 'shut the fuck up you faggot' and left him lying in the yard at the back of the Jar behind the empty kegs with his ribs broke and his head kicked and pulped like a beetroot. Kenneth looked the other way. He didn't want trouble, certainly not with those two little thugs, but didn't want a corpse in his yard neither, so he hitched his saggy trousers up over his barkeep belly and rang for an ambulance. Callum got scooped up and taken to the infirmary where they wired his jaw – to remind him to keep his mouth shut.

After he got discharged, Callum went back home, and for a long time, he never went out, and he lived on spaghetti hoops and sloppy instant whip, but he missed Pop-Tarts. Sycorax said they might get a liquidiser, but they didn't even though she had the money; she was flush back then. Windfall, she said. Six weeks later, when the wires were removed, the first thing Callum did was two strawberry Pop-Tarts and burned his mouth on the cheap synthetic jam. The pastry was sharp as daggers in the soft cunt of his mouth.

Callum was a worrier, his broad-bean forehead creased with it. He was worried sick about going back to work, his usual *place* of work, the yard behind the Nightjar – where he got his jaw broken. He tried. He went down there one afternoon and got as far as the swing door. He glimpsed Kenneth in his elasticated-waist trousers leaning on the bar reading the *Daily Mirror*: COLLISION COURSE FOR WAR!* Callum's guts churned. He flattened back against the wall, screwed up his eyes until asteroids came, and he blasted a few in his mind's eye while his quaking spasm subsided, then he went home.

Sycorax, the old motherwitch, was lolling on the settee in diaphanous *eau de nil*, drinking tequila and watching quiz shows on her new telly. She threw back her head and laughed.

'Maybe you need another direction,' she said. 'Join the army, my boy. Fight for Queen and Country in this little war they're all talking about.'

OFF TO WAR BY JUMBO!† Callum didn't think he was stupid enough for the army – he saw himself as more of a strategist. Being a fighter pilot with the Fleet Air Arm would be a fine thing; he'd be the best at that, blasting enemy planes out of the sky. If only heights didn't make him feel so peculiar.

*'COLLISION COURSE FOR WAR!', *Daily Mirror*, 5 April 1982.

†'OFF TO WAR BY JUMBO!', *The Sun*, 7 April 1982. (A complete fabrication: troops were not flown off to fight by jumbo jet. Frustrated by the lack of information concerning the Task Force sailing to the Falklands, *The Sun* occasionally invented news, and was in any case, rarely able to resist the opportunity of a cracking headline.)

For a time then, the fear pivoting in his gut kept him home. Some of the old men from the Jar started coming to the flat, knocking quietly, looking over their shoulders, invisible to everyone except Sycorax. She'd see them in their shabby anoraks and zip-up cardies. She'd let them in and take their money. Before Callum's jaw got broken, the money went on Asteroids. Now he works from home, and she takes the money and says it all goes on Pop-Tarts. He thinks they used to pay more, and now they pay less. He puzzles over what is the opposite of inflation. State of the nation?

Ascension Island, April 1982

Dearest Mama,

The good news is that your Georg lives still in this world. *Dios sea loado*. I am captured by British armies, and except for them shooting dead one poor man called Arturo or Artuso, we have been treated well enough, though they kick us and call us stinkers.

When they came to South Georgia, we were all herded together, the scrap workers and the defeated military, over a hundred, most of them so young, so *very* young, just boys without yet hair on their chins. We were all put on board a tanker, *Tidespring*. It clanked and wallowed, few were not sick with the constant ploughing down and up, and we have been taken to Ascension Island. Get my atlas off the shelf, Mama, put your finger on the place, and I will feel it; I will know you are thinking of me. They say this island is a paradise, but we see only the concrete of the military base. From here, I cannot tell if we will be shipped to Grand Britannia as prisoners of the war or sent home. I pray for home.

Your son, Georg.

We Are All Falklanders Now*

At last, Woody was alone. Aloneness soaked into him like liniment. For once, he had the flat to himself, and there was no sound but the rattle of his typewriter as words unspooled from his wounded, wound-up, clock-spring mind. He was a two-finger typist, and he typed in ragtime, and the rhythm soothed his soul. He was writing a play based on Marcel Duchamp's *Large Glass: The Bride Stripped Bare by Her Bachelors, Even.* It was supposed to be an essay for the compulsory, but arguably pointless, Critical Studies part of his course, but it had morphed. He was writing dialogue for the bachelor apparatus, a complicated exchange between the nine malic moulds...

Another rattle interjected. A contrapuntal clattering of the letterbox. He sighed, picked up his cigarette and went to the door.

Outside there was a rat-featured child, one of the smaller ones in a dress with a bright yellow smiley faced sunshine on the front. Her own face above was streaked with dirt.

'Is Petra in?' she asked.

'No.'

'Can I wait for her?'

'No.'

'That's mean.'

---

*'WE ARE ALL FALKLANDERS NOW', *The Times*, 5 April 1982.

The child sat down with her legs crossed, exposing the gusset of her underpants. She scowled blackly. Woody stepped back and tried to close the door, but her knee was in the way.

'Look, what do you want?'

'Petra said that if I was sad about anything, I could talk to her. And I am very sad today because of Mungo.'

Woody was pricked by a desire to meddle in someone else's misery as a distraction from his own. For weeks now, he had been imagining himself lost in a labyrinth. By day he wrote of Duchamp's *Large Glass*, and by night, he dreamt of being trapped inside it. Each night, in the recurring dream, he is imprisoned in its frame, caught between the two walls of cracked glass and wretched to the point of dementia with the commotion and urgency of the lower part: the region of the bachelor. His head ricochets with the jangle, shriek, gnash and rasp of the grinders, the shots, the pistons. Stan is there, in the dream, in the lower segment, and in his element. Stan is properly male, malic, a malic mould. In the cemetery of uniforms and liveries, he is the Station Master; 'Gas, boys, gas,' he shouts with his chest puffed out. Woody dreams that he sheds his own uniform (flunky) like a skin and trades his sex cylinder for the chance to slither up into the bride's domain where all physical relations are stalled intentions. The bride is a wasp. Sometimes he dreams he wraps the wasp in a veil, sometimes, *he* is the fluctuating veil, sometimes he is a spool of invisible mending thread, and the thread spools out of his belly button, or the spiracles of his thorax, it spools out damp and white, drying to a wire that binds him tight... His mind spooled.

'Well?' said the child.

He knew he must get away. Away from the glass. Away from Lovelace, from the other two and their intellectual vacuity. He was sure that that was what stifled his creativity. It must be. But right at that very instant, being an agony uncle might serve as a diversion.

'Alright, you can come in, but don't touch any of my stuff.'

She followed him down to the kitchen, and he made her a glass of squash. She sat on one of the crocodile chairs, swinging her legs and wiping her nose on the back of her hand.

'When will Petra be back?'

'Don't know.'

'Where's she gone?'

'I'm afraid I don't know that either.'

'Are you Petra's boyfriend?'

'No, just a friend.'

'Is the other one Petra's boyfriend? The big boy with the sticky-up hair?'

'Stan, no, he's not. We just all share the flat.'

'Is there anything to eat?'

He checked the bread for mould and made her a peanut butter sandwich. She bolted the middle and left the crusts.

'So, you're just friends?' she asked between mouthfuls and without a trace of irony.

There was no point in saying they lived in an infernal triangle of unsuitable attraction, repression, and resentment, and the last thing they were likely to do was to be friendly or honest with each other. So he sat opposite and asked:

'Who do you live with?'

'With Mam and my sister Tessa.'

'Can't you talk to them about being sad?'

'Mam's out at work – she's always at work – and Tessa's just stoopid. She mostly cries all the time, and sometimes she makes her legs bleed.'

'What about your dad?'

'He lives over on Dalton Walk with his other wife and their new baby, and she says that if I knock their door one more time, she will get me taken away and put into care. So, Petra said—'

'Okay, okay. Um, I don't know your name.'

'Ruby,' she said like she shouldn't have to remind him.

'Ruby. What are you sad about?'

'About Mungo. They stabbed him. And...' Tears began to dribble down her cheeks, leaving snail trails of cleanish skin. Woody looked around helplessly, wishing they had tissues or kitchen paper.

'Who is Mungo?'

'My friend.'

Shit was getting serious here. Maybe this Mungo was a stuffed toy or just imaginary, but what if he was one of the other kids, lying in a pool of blood, dead or dying. Jeez, what atrocity had this child witnessed? He would dramatize it, perhaps in iambic pentameter.

'Don't touch anything,' he ordered and darted off to the bathroom for bog roll. After she'd blown her nose and gulped some of the squash, he asked tentatively,

'Is Mungo, like, real?'

'Course he's *real*. He's my friend, and now he's dead, and I hate them, I hate them all. Those boys had him trapped in an old suitcase, and they said he was their prisoner. A prisoner of war or something. They were kicking the suitcase, and poor Mungo was going wild at first, howling, and I tried to save him, but they pinned me down, and I bit Samir, so him and his brother kicked me in the ribs, then they sat on me and said Mungo had to be executed. They said I had to watch, as punishment for trying to help the prisoner escape. They undid the clips on the case and opened it, and Mungo was lying on his side panting with his little mouth open to meow, but no sound came, and there was blood on his fur, down his chin. Then they stabbed him in his side with a penknife, and he yowled a bit, then he didn't, and they took it in turns to stab him over and over so that all his insides came out. They kept on stabbing him and saying he was an Argy.'

'A cat? That black and white one that shits on the balconies?'

MAY 1982

Dear Mum: Swarming with Flies

Dear Mum,

Thank you for the birthday present which I have now eventually got. There was no one in when they tried to deliver it, and it doesn't seem to be the norm here to leave parcels with the neighbours or propped up in the front porch (I guess it's *not* Hertfordshire), so I had to get the bus down to the city to go to the sorting office, and the first time I went, I had forgotten to take any ID with me. Apparently, the card pushed through the letterbox doesn't count. But anyway, *thank you!* I am sure I will be glad of a dressing gown when the weather is a bit cooler. It's sweltering here. Sorry not to write a longer letter, I'm pushed for time with a deadline looming for my Critical Studies essay on Marcel Duchamp's *Large Glass*. There's no news here in any event!

Love to you, and cordial regards to the stepfather.

Petra

Dear Mum,

What the fuck were you thinking? A dressing gown? Please send the receipt so I can get yet another bus down to Marks & Sparks for a refund and have the cash instead to buy something remotely useful. Must dash. I've some guff to write, and if I don't get a decent grade for it, I may have to come home.

Love to you and NOT to that old pervert you are shacked up with.

Petra

P.S. I've just seen the funniest thing ever. Down by the phone box there's a dead cat with a stick up its arse, like a kebab.

Petra put the first letter in an envelope, and the second, with some regret, she screwed up and tossed onto the floor. There was no point in being gratuitously honest. Her mind was fingering the other thing that had happened while she was on her way home, when she was walking up the rise from the bus stop. It was probably nothing, but it felt like having forgotten something, or misunderstood something, or missed the point. But it was nothing, right?

Radiation Man was back. After someone bonfired the old settee, he'd disappeared for a while, but now he was back, and he had new furniture: a chair on wheels, like a typist might sit on in an office. It was broken, and one of the wheels was missing, but he looked pleased with it anyway. Still in a tinfoil cap, he was scooting about with a wide grin splitting his face. And he'd got a fridge down there too, only not plugged into anything and half-covered in black mould. He was watching a television made out of an empty crisp box with a wire coat-hanger stuck in the top for an aerial.

'Have yer seen the noos?' he called out to her.

Petra smiled and shook her head.

'Well, there's a killer whale in the South Atlantic Ocean. He's called Ada, and he's bigger than a continent, and he's a man-eater with a liking for fries. Don't say I didn't warn yer.'

It was the most coherent thing Petra had ever heard him say. Then a hulk of a woman in a funky-striped imitation fur coat came puffing up from the direction of the shop with a plastic bottle of Mr Khalil's bootleg voddy and two paper cups.

Radiation Man got up and gave her his seat. She settled herself like a goose over eggs.

Too hot for a coat like that, thought Petra, she must be boiling.

'Oi! Princess,' the woman shouted. She stared intently at Petra; her eyes were glittering dark slits in her broad, thread-veined face. 'You mind how you go now.'

Petra felt a chill as if the bones of her thoughts had been dipped in liquid nitrogen, deep-frozen, and splintered into shards.

A New Word Enters the Lexicon

As the British Task Force reaches the South Atlantic, diplomatic resolution looks increasingly unlikely. On 2 May 1982, a deadly game of Battleships commences. Costs of the Falklands War will include the loss of over nine hundred lives: 649 Argentinians ('The Argies') 255 British Military Personnel ('Our Lads') and 3 Falklanders, civilians killed accidentally by friendly fire. One small payoff is the enrichment of our vocabulary.*

Exocet: A missile to destroy. Very effective when launched from a Dassault-Breguet Super Étendard, if you happen to have one to hand. But you can launch an Exocet from land, from a ship, or a plane, a helicopter, or submarine; they are so versatile.

Exocet is French for leaping fish. Sometimes they leap right out of the water and get stranded in boats. Boats that could have been elsewhere should have been. Not in an imaginary circle drawn on a map, a two-hundred-mile exclusion zone.

The etymology of the word Exocet points to the Latin: *Exocoetus* or maybe the Greek: *Exokōitos*. Either way, a fish that literally 'sleeps outside'. A fish that eschews the cover of

---

*Other non-Exocet missiles were also in play, and the ships sunk were HMS *Ardent* (21 May), HMS *Antelope* (23 May), HMS *Coventry* (25 May) and RFA *Sir Galahad* (8 June). We got twenty of theirs. Hoorah.

waves or sheets for its coitus. A promiscuous fish, one that sleeps around.

Funding? *Il Banco Ambrosiano,* the bankers of God, had a hand in that. The French did the inventing and the making but later withheld supply and withdrew technical support to avoid diplomatic hot water. Peru took delivery but sued for peace. The Argies pushed the button. Oh, we had them too. Our hands were not clean. Who can you trust?

In the Falklands, Exocets were used against the British Task Force, sinking ships, destroying equipment, and killing men, including cooks. Fourteen naval cooks were killed in the war – or conflict – if you prefer. Fourteen.

An AM39 air-launched Exocet missile destroyed HMS *Sheffield* on 4 May. Did the warhead of the missile actually explode? Five separate salvage inspections were made. The findings were inconclusive. Next, on 25 May, an Exocet sunk the 15,000-ton merchant ship SS *Atlantic Conveyor,* and then on 12 June, HMS *Glamorgan* was hit.

Dave Keane's brother was a cook in the Royal Navy.

So, This Julian Bloke?

Saturday Morning. Woody had been up since early. His Critical Studies essay, which had been late, was now disastrously late. He sat at his campaign desk, fingers dancing over the typewriter keys, perfecting the soliloquy of the lovely Chocolate Grinder, his second favourite character. He was still, in his dreams, trapped in Duchamp's glass, but he was never the Chocolate Grinder. `One is lonely, two is company, three's a crowd.` Or maybe `three's company, and two's a bore`... Hearing the others beginning to stir, he opened his door, perversely leaving it ajar to be purposely pissed off. He wanted to be sure, absolutely sure, that he could no longer stay. He felt emptied out by the atmosphere of Lovelace Flats, by the smell of decay and death. It was a Sodom and Gomorrah of squalor, a condemned and irredeemable circle of hell. Its hapless denizens beetled about, pursuing their petty crimes and penny-foolish vices, oblivious to their predicament: they were being inexorably sucked towards the plughole. This ugly truth of Lovelace was seemingly invisible to everyone in their medicinal blinkers – everyone except maybe the shouty psycho who camped out below the flats. And besides, Woody was sick of the noise; there was always someone screaming, doors slamming, music blaring, dogs barking. Inside was no better; he was sapped by the bickering, sick of tripping over Petra's tart-trotters, the stench of Stan's jars of turps, sick of their constant piss-taking, obdurate childishness. Obdurate – good word. Must try to slot it in somewhere.

He glanced up to see Stan passing his door, yawning, scratching his balls, wearing nothing but a pair of underpants he must have had since he was twelve. Not lucky pants or Saturday pants. Just old pants. Although it was another spear in his St Sebastian side, Woody was glad to have seen those underpants one last time before he left. Stan had a good body, sturdy and durable. Though what was the point of durability when you were whooshing towards the plughole?

The toilet flushed, and Stan banged on the bathroom door.

'Move it, Slap. I've got a match this morning.'

The door opened, and out came a bloke in a brown suit; he was in need of a shave but otherwise presentable. Woody had a perfect view, a vertical sliver of the encounter at the end of the hallway. He relished the vicarious thrill of an awkward moment as Stan and the stranger were each surprised by the proximity of the other. Stan recovered first.

'Morning, Squire!' he leered.

'Ur, Petra said...'

Woody quietly eased himself out of his chair, inched round his desk and went on toes through to the kitchen, itching to see how this played out, loathing himself for giving in to his spinsterish curiosity. Closer up, Woody could see that the natty-three-piece bloke had remarkably bloodshot eyes and wore a single gold earring. He was fishing around in the sink for something. He selected a glass, rinsed it, and drank a long draught of tap water.

'Are you...?' asked Woody.

'Julian, ah, er, a friend of Petra's. She said it would be, er...'

'Alright?'

Julian gazed around the kitchen. Woody watched him taking in the modernist sketches taped all around the grubby magnolia walls, the dying cheese plant, murky jars of turps, the dubious papier mâché mobiles hanging from the ceiling, Stan's pushbike with Petra's washing draped over the crossbar. There was gone-off milk in almost empty bottles, shoes, crumbs, overdue library books, a pan of congealed vegetable something. The kitchen was pretentiously arty and archly squalid. This was no way to live.

'Er, well, I'm running late.' Julian said. He rinsed the glass again and looked for somewhere clean to put it. Defeated, he put it back in the sink and left. Cuban heels.

When he had gone, Petra appeared, wrapped in a vermillion silk kimono pinched from the wardrobe at the polytechnic drama department. She looked like death; Woody thought he had seen more wholesome-looking zombies. Her face was both pale and blotchy at the same time, her eyes were dull, and her hair, a rat's nest at the back. She smelt cheap. Woody eyed her with little interest and less sympathy. Neither of them spoke.

Stan, now in trackie bottoms and a jumper his dear old nan had knitted, started banging about, getting breakfast, and the needling and bickering commenced like it always did. It was impossible to concentrate, impossible to write. Woody was quite sure he needed cleanliness, blankness, solitude, calm. He couldn't live like this.

'Make me a coffee, Stanie,' Petra mewed.

'Make it yourself, I ain't got time. And who was that? I thought we all agreed, no random overnighters. After what happened last time. You agreed.'

'He gave me a lift home and – can't you eat those quietly?'

'Uh-uh, cornflakes,' he said with his mouth full. 'So, he drove here? But he must've been shitfaced. He still looked absolutely shitfaced just now. What time d'you get home?'

'Back off, Mum.'

'And who is he? What's he do for a living? I assume he's got a job. If he's got a car, he must have a job. That stands to reason. He's not one of us, suit like that.'

'It's just a suit.'

'Well, he looked like he'd stepped out of Burton's window. Or does he do a bit of modelling for the catalogues?' With milk dripping from his spoon to the floor, Stan posed like a mannequin. 'Ooh! Something *off the peg* for you, sir?'

Petra mumbled something.

'He's a what?' Stanley exploded half-chewed cornflakes over the table.

'Wine merchant,' muttered Petra.

'Ha! Well, I banged on the door and shouted, "Move it, Slap!" coz I thought it was *you* in the bog and I needed to get in there, and then out comes lover boy – did he have a big dong?'

'Adequate.'

'That all?'

'You know.' She shrugged.

'Wine frigging merchant? Are you for real, girl?' Stan kissed her on the top of her head and picked up his kit bag. 'Laters, Woody.'

Woody inhaled that slightly rank smell of not entirely clean sports kit, layered with Stanley's usual fragrance of soap and turps. Another thorn. Leaving Petra at the cornflake-spattered kitchen table with her head in her hands, Woody went back to his room and put a fresh piece of paper in his typewriter.

Dear Mr Eastwatch,

Re: Critical Studies Essay

Duchamp's Large Glass: La Mariée Mise à Nu par ses Célibataires, Même is elitist, obscure, self-indulgent, full of puns and double entendres. Duchamp incorporates elements of time, chance, skill, but ultimately the work is futile and meaningless. It is a joke, a very clever in-joke, but nevertheless, a joke. My 'essay' is likewise an exercise in futility. I have made excuses for the delay for several weeks now, and I am aware this has tried your patience. But at last, I can reveal the true reason for the lateness: like Duchamp himself, I have been waiting for dust to settle. But now I realise, even dust cannot settle here.

Yours faithfully
John Woodford (Woody)

He put the letter in a large manila envelope with his magnum opus, a play that should have been an essay, and began to pack.

The Plan: In Which Callum Devises a Brilliant Scheme to Prove He Did Not Grass on Mr Keane, and Considers His Choice of Weapon

Just as some people move their lips when reading, never having developed the capacity to make the words in their heads, *in abstraction*, so Callum McCandless moved his lips when he was thinking. No sooner a thought was thought, but quite unchecked, it became a word on his rather full ruby lips. It might escape as a faint sibilant hiss, or a mumbling, something like prayer. At other times, a stream of agitation stuttered through like ticker tape.

'Loose lips sink ships,' said Mrs Beasley, from Number 18, giving him the evil eye.

He thought it was a tongue-twister, but apparently, it wasn't. Word had got about, about him taking a kicking and why. They all thought he deserved it – and more.

'Shut yer face, stupid old woman, it's Exocet missiles that sink ships,' he mumbled.

He'd seen it in the paper: GOTCHA* and wished he could get his hands on one of them Exocets. First, he would blast old Mrs Beasley with her lizardy skin. KABOOM! Next would be the surly bitch at the DHSS. KABOOM! He wanted to claim sick pay, but the bitch had said no because he didn't have a job, so he couldn't be off sick. He got flustered, swore at her, and stormed out. It was hard for him to explain that for a man

---

*'GOTCHA', *The Sun*, 4 May 1982 ('Our Lads Sink Gunboat and Hole Cruiser' was the knee-jerk response to the sinking of the ARA *General Belgrano* with the loss of 323 lives.)

who supplements his dole by sucking other men's cocks, having your jaw wired for six weeks is an economic disaster.

~

Callum needs to prove that he is not a grass. He needs a plan. His lips move, spittle gathers in the corners of his mouth, a plan forms. He will be just *like* Mr Keane. Not with the tattoos and the running and weird shit, but he will kill someone. Like Keane did. LOCAL HERO, easy-peasy. Those skinheads from the Jar will be open-mouthed with admiration. Their precious pool cues will wilt limp as dicks when they see what he is capable of: CLEVER BASTARD! Callum isn't scared of getting caught. Getting caught is a necessary part of the plan; he *wants* everyone to know what he has done. Prison will be fine. Prison will be clean and warm, he'll wear nice tracksuits, get proper meals with pudding and custard.

He needs a weapon. For a copycat killing, it should be a van because that's what Keane used. Keane 'borrowed' the van that belonged to the skinny old Chinaman who used to work in the dry cleaners that went out of business. But Callum hasn't got a van. Anyway, he never learned to drive. So, he rules out a van, then he rules out a gun. Only gun he's got is the BB gun for taking potshots at that manky cat.

Stabbing is the way to go. Something sharp.

Sharp Objects (*n*)

Sycorax's tongue, for starters. All the pocketknives in all the pockets of all the boys on the estate. Admittedly, some blunted with carving obscenities and names on doors. Sometimes they practice knife throwing against the wall, and then the points get dull or snap off altogether from hitting concrete, just to the left or the right of their mark. Above, below, too high, too slow. Bullseye.

Hypodermic needles. New ones are sharper than ones that've been passed around. And they are. Passed around and shared, used and reused, because nobody knows any better. There's hepatitis, and you can catch that from dirty needles, but hey, you've gotta die of something.

Mr and Mrs Sharpe, 51 Dalton Walk: he is a whining drunk, she is partially deaf from where he hit her across the head for not listening.

Old Mr Sharpe on Garnett, the first Mr Sharpe's uncle, the one that's allergic to cats. Dapper bachelor, 'an invert', they say. Keeps himself to himself, more or less.

Razor blades. That's what Ruby's sad sister cuts her legs with.

What else is sharp?

Broken glass. Sharp suits. Chest pains, that's what killed stinky old Mr Kite. Swords and screwdrivers, machetes and axes, sewing needles, drawing pins. Scissors.

Kitchen knives, lying quietly in the drawers in kitchens in flats on each of the walks: Babbage, Dalton, Rutherford, Faraday, Garnett. Every kitchen's got knives. Sycorax keeps hers in the drawer next to the sink.

Choose one.

The Plan: In Which Callum Selects a Victim for His Non-identical Copycat-Killing

Now that Villiers the bastard has gone, who (apart from Callum's mother) does everyone hate?

Callum hears the old-timers saying that the neighbourhood has gone to the dogs. Used to be, the timers said, you could put signs up, ROOM TO LET: NO BLACKS, NO IRISH. Then it was NO PETS, NO SMOKERS, NO DHSS (City Council rules on subletting notwithstanding). But allowing in students? That is beyond the pale. That's what the timers say: BEYOND THE PALE. And Callum doesn't really know what it means. But he supposes there should now be signs saying NO STUDENTS, NO VEGETARIANS, NO POSH TWATS. Those students, they come here with their lah-di-dah accents and their oh-look-at-me weird hairstyles, their jazz music and vegetarian food, oooh jazz. They think they're fitting in to some authentic city life, but they are SORE THUMBS. They think they are slumming it, think it's hilarious slumming it, here in our flats. They hoot to one another at the tops of their over-privileged windpipes. They march down to Mr Khalil's shop and ask him for muesli and *The Guardian. The* fucking *Guardian*. They sit in the Nightjar smoking rollies and ya-ya-yaing. They are so FUCKING IRONIC about everything. And no, Callum is not sure what ironic means.

In his twisted mind, an idea takes shape. He spits out his intentions in a staccato of spittle: clear Lovelace Flats of these lazy parasites. Kill just one, and then they will all think twice about coming here for cheap bloody housing and free bloody underfloor heating.

He thinks he will kill the student next door, the handsome pretentious one in the hat, the one that plays the dreadful music with no words to it, just a screeching wail of brass in rhythms that twist and disappear. Just thinking about him, Callum gets a stiffy, and he has to shut his eyes and activate the hyperspace mechanism until it passes. He mulls this over for a couple of days, and then his intended moves out. Callum sees him loading his desk and his suitcases and his saxophone into a van, and with his hat pushed right back on his head, he drives away.

Not wanting to tackle the bigger boy, the one with the leery grin, he decides to kill *her* instead. The one with the clickety-clickety high-heeled shoes. She's weak and small. Easy meat. When Sycorax is busy with a punter or sleeping off a skinful, he will slip out, wait in the stairwell with a knife, drop onto next door's balcony, break into their flat. Wait for her; clickety-clickety. She is a bad girl. Little slut.

Harpo Objects (*v*)

They went to the pub, just Petra and Harpo. Harpo was her usual self, but Petra felt awkward; she found Harpo very intense. She thought that Harpo thought that she was silly: a silly bitch, airhead, fluffer. Petra was sure that Harpo had seen her coming home from her job at the wine bar, in heels. Tottering up the road from the bus stop on three-and-a-half inches of patriarchal subjugation. She anticipated a lecture.

Harpo ordered a pint of bitter, Petra, the same. The jukebox loaded the next record. It was so quiet in there that Petra could hear the mechanical arm collect the vinyl, swing across and load it onto the turntable, and she could hear the slight burr of pickup at the start of the track before the blather of pop. Harpo scowled. Petra danced on the inside, thinking of her new friend Celeste, who drank white wine spritzers. Celeste, who was 'from' here. Celeste, who was real. Celeste and Harpo; how different they were, how much they would loathe each other on principle – and they were both hot on matters of principle.

Harpo led the way to the nearest of the slightly sticky tables, its wonkiness mitigated with a folded beermat shoved under one leg. The pair of skinheads who hog the pool table were wearing matching Union Jack T-shirts. They acknowledged Harpo with a nod.

'Alright.'

'Alright.'

Petra was relieved that Harpo would not need to fight them again. Today, Harpo was engaged in a different battle:

'So, I got the bus down to the city and went to the Army Recruitment Office—' she said.

Petra's eyes widened with surprise. She knew Harpo to be a communist, republican, atheist, man-hating lesbian, and lazy drama student.

'—you know they've set up a portacabin in the market square?'

Petra nodded.

'Well, they're idiots, fucking arseholes and idiots.'

Petra nodded.

Harpo rooted about in her canvas holdall, got out a tin of tobacco, papers, Zippo. Placed them on the table, lined them up.

'So, I told them I want to join the Paras, and they said—' she took a swig of her pint, her top lip moustachioed with froth. '—and they said, I can't because I have tits! TITS!'

The two skinheads, cues in hand, turned and stared slack-jawed as Harpo shouted. Kenneth looked up from his newspaper. The old man in the corner with the bottle of Mackeson and the rancid Jack Russell terrier, he fixed Harpo with his rheumy eye, a perplexed look on his face; perhaps he had misheard. His hand fluttered; he looked as if he might ask her to repeat what she just said. The dog smirked.

Harpo glared at Petra, waiting for something. Petra was flipping beer mats off the edge of the table, a fidgety thing. She was unready to speak. She had not anticipated this.

'How dare they?' Harpo prompted.

'How *very* dare they!' added Petra lamely.

Petra imagined Harpo wearing military boots and khaki, her asymmetric haircut trimmed equally short on both sides.

She didn't doubt for even one nanosecond that Harpo could drive a tank or jump out of a plane. She didn't doubt that Harpo could and *would* bayonet an Argy in the guts; thrust and twist until coils of glistening sausage intestines spilled out. But really? She thought most *blokes* were shitting themselves in case this whole Malvinas/Falklands thing escalated, and the government started calling up the reservists. The next step would be conscription.

~

But Petra was wrong; she did not see how things were. The whole nation was infected with patriotism. BRITAIN WILL FIGHT!*

*'BRITAIN WILL FIGHT!', *Daily Mail*, April 1982.

Buenos Aires, May 1982

Repatriate: (transitive verb). Send back something or someone that had no business being where it was. The thing returned has no agency, obviously.

'Enough, Mama, enough. Always the fuss. I'm going out.'

Is it not enough for her that I am home?

Hands deep in pockets, collar up, head down, I walk through the city. Turn right behind the Colón opera house into a side street, narrow, litter-choked, and walk towards the indoor market. A thin dog going in the same direction pisses methodically in each doorway. If only international territories were that easy.

The café is open, still open. Still the same. Silvio looks up from his newspaper just a fraction too late for anyone to mistake the gesture for politeness.

'Georg,' he says as if I have been nowhere. He hoists up his trousers and flicks a cloth over his shoulder. He turns to the espresso machine, hissing and spitting with malevolence, grinding with obstinate grudge. Silvio spends his working life turning his back on people.

Two old men in identical jerseys are hunched over a game of chess. They look up.

'Georg.'

'Georg.'

'Ernesto, Gomez. Who's losing today?'

'Everyone.'

Silvio pushes a coffee across the counter, the cup too full, the coffee too bitter. But still, it's good to be home.

Heatwave

Heatwave: When high pressure systems move slowly, or hardly at all. According to the Met Office, three consecutive days (min) when the recorded temperature (max) exceeds HTT (heatwave temperature thresholds). For the East Midlands, this is twenty-seven degrees Celsius. Heatwaves are held responsible for raised levels of violent crime, increased morbidity rates, and clichés such as 'resentment simmers' and 'tensions come to the boil'.

Bank Holiday Monday. The weather was a novelty that, after only two days, had worn off. The city was a dustbowl with heat radiating off buildings and buses and tarmac. Summer had caught us on the hop, and no one had yet shopped for shorts and flip-flops. Boys had their shirts off, chests pinking. Old ladies drooped with bra straps slipping down flabby arms. The air was suffused with a faint stink of perspiration and popsicles. Above it all, the mocking blue skies of expensive holiday destinations were an absurdity here in the East Midlands.

Woody, now living alone above a piano shop, returned to Lovelace, ostensibly to collect his mail but also to avoid a lecherous piano tuner called Victor. Since moving out, he had progressed to fully-fledged writer's block and insomnia. Despite the heat, he was dressed in black, like a cloud. His only concession to the glare of the day was a pair of wraparound shades. He found Stan and Petra bickering.

'Are you being a tiresome shrew?' he asked her.

'He started it.'

'If you say so.'

'Pub?'

'Yeah.'

'Nightjar?'

'Yeah.'

'No.'

'No?'

'Where then?'

'Let's get out of this. Up to the ridge. Catch some breeze.'

'Sherwood.'

It's not far. Too far to walk in the heat, so three amigos reunited waited for a bus, and with time to spare, they sat on a bench reading red tops: THE PAPER THAT SUPPORTS OUR BOYS* and WOT A SCORCHER!† A thin old woman walked towards them; she had a rat-like underbite and dead eyes and walked as if balancing on a tightrope, heel to toe, arms held out from her sides. As she got closer, just a couple of feet away, she hawked and spat at them.

'Pinkos,' she said.

They boarded the grumbling, fume-belching number 42, winding its stop-start way the last few stops uphill before it U-turned for its exhilarating, freewheeling descent back down to the city. The bus was almost empty, and Petra, Woody and Stan were each silent with their own thoughts, enduring the heat and the tedium of the journey.

~

High up on the ridge above the haze of the city, two wasps investigated three pints of cider. Petra examined the freckles ap-

---

*'THE PAPER THAT SUPPORTS OUR BOYS', *The Sun*. This strapline was used every day from 11 May 1982.

†'WOT A SCORCHER!', *East Midlands Gazette*, 1 June 1982.

pearing on her pale arms, Stan wiped his mouth with the back of his hand, Woody drummed his fingers. He thought he had missed them, even Petra. He was wrong.

'Well,' said Petra, 'Would you rather... be beautiful and stupid, or ugly but clever?'

Stan spluttered: 'Oh, you are such a girl. That is such a girl question. Clever and ugly obviously, right, Woods?'

Petra rolled her eyes. Woody could guess what she was thinking. Something about how being pretty was a smart choice. For Stan, beauty was always inanimate: line, form, colour, tone, blah, blah. He could be so literal.

Woody pushed his hat further back on his head, stroked his long nose.

'No. It's not a girl question. I would choose stupid every day.' He had their undivided. 'If you're stupid, you probably don't even know you're stupid. But if you were ugly, you'd always already know you were ugly, and especially so if you were clever. I would never choose to be ugly. It's more than skin deep, man.'

Silence.

From behind his sunglasses, Woody watched. He watched Stan, not ugly, but unbeautiful: muscular, wholesome, artless. And Petra, basking in the lengthening rays, glancing back at him from under her lashes and checking herself in the reflection. Why was attraction so often tragically misdirected? Maybe drink would blot them out. The one he couldn't stop dreaming about, and the other one who was a bit in love with him. Maybe drink or death?

Woody narrowed his invisible eyes. 'My turn,' he said. 'Would you rather... know *when* you are going to die or know *how* you are going to die?'

'Oooh, that's macabre.' Petra hunched up her shoulders as if iced water had trickled unexpectedly between the blades.

Stan picked up his pint, gulped cider, and belched. 'Your round, I believe, Mr Woodford,' he said. 'And nuts. Would you rather... have ordinary salted or dry roasted?'

They laughed, even Woody, and banged on the table: 'Nuts, nuts, nuts, nuts!' There was no consensus on the nuts, so Woody went to the bar for both.

In the cool panelled interior of the Sherwood Arms, with its yellowed prints and military memorabilia of long-ago wars and eternally memorialised men, all the windows were open, and he could still hear Stan and Petra discussing the least worst knowledge of death to live with, how you could use it to take risks, and how, conversely, it would haunt your living days with the inevitability, and the dread.

'What if you knew it would happen tomorrow?'

'Or tonight.'

'Supposing you know you are going to drown?'

'You'd never dare swim. Even taking a bath might be sketchy.'

'Is that your excuse?'

'What if you knew you'd make ninety? You'd be confident you could do anything.'

'Or an even hundred.'

'Or die in bed? How could you sleep?'

'What if you knew you would die of a broken heart?'

'You haven't got one.'

'I have too.'

'What if you wanted to die, but you couldn't?'

'Supposing you know it's got to be a violent end?'

'Murdered. No, tortured and murdered?'

'Exsanguination, starvation, sepsis, suicide?'

On the other side of the bar, a television screen relayed images from the other side of the world. For weeks, there has been no footage of the Falklands War, but now, at the beginning of the end, borrowed satellites beamed images home. As he waited to be served, Woody watched, appalled. A terrain of black rock and white frost, dark-eyed broken men weighed down with the shame of defeat, trudging in line with their arms raised high: prisoners of war. And following them, two boys weighed down with equipment and weapons and responsibility.

It was all so impossibly far away.

JUNE 1982

Fugitive

From the Latin, fugutivus *– to flee, as in 'tempus fugit'. Fugitive (noun) person fleeing from something: could be jurisdiction, imprisonment, slavery, war. A person beyond custody, 'at large', 'on the lam', 'out of pocket'. Fugitive (adjective) fleeting, hard to pin down. In art, a pigment that won't last, perhaps due to exposure to the light, perhaps just short-lived, as in 'tempus fugit'.*

Petra got home from the wine bar, and drinks afterwards, a bit pissed and didn't notice anything wrong with the front door. Stumbling down the still uncarpeted stairs, she pulled up short at the sight of Stan, armed with a cricket bat gripped in white knuckles. He saw her and lunged in the same instant, adrenalin kicking in fractionally before his brain. He slumped.

'It's you,' he said.

'Shit, Stan, yeah, it's me. I live here, remember? What's up? I thought you were going to give me a clattering.'

'Did you see the door?' he said.

'What door?'

'The front door, for fuck's sake. Are you blind?'

'Drunk.'

'They just busted in. Two of them. Police in riot gear.'

'Police?'

'In riot gear. Two of them.'

'Fuck!'

'You're damned straight, "fuck!" I was just enjoying a cuppa and a crafty bifter, watching a documentary on coal mining in Pennsylvania because it was the only thing on telly *not* about the bloody war. Do you know there's a coal seam runs under the Atlantic, all the way from Wales? It's the same coal.'

'So what?'

'Then there was banging, and the door jamb splintering, two thugs in black coming downstairs, busting in the kitchen. Shouting, "Hands above your head! Hands where I can see them! David Keane? Are you David Keane? Is he here?" And I was jibbering like, like... a jibbering idiot, and saying no, I am not David fucking Keane. Well, I didn't actually say "fucking" coz, well, you don't, do you? Not to the police. But I wanted to.'

'Hell's bells! Did you piss yourself?'

'It was a close thing. Luckily, I had just gone in the ad break. Then they calmed down a bit and wanted to see identification, so I showed them my library card, then they started calling me *Sir*, and–'

Stan came to an abrupt stop. He dropped his eyes.

'Jeez, girl, where you been hiding those legs?'

Petra touched the hem of her skirt and stumbled towards him; she was just at that affectionate stage of inebriation. They stood nose to nose, the bat separating them like a chaperone. Petra breathed in that special mix – soap, turps, old sports kit, and as her ribs rose and her lungs filled, the moment was gone like helium. She turned away, flicked on the light, a bare sixty-watt bulb. Her feet ached. She sat on one of the man-eating crocodile print chairs in the kitchen.

'So, who's this Keane?' she asked, picking up the thread of what had gone before.

'Dunno, but he used to live here. This is his last known address. He's escaped from prison. Some prison up north, and apparently, he's gone over the wall and legged it. He was doing time for manslaughter in HMP something-or-other. *Absconded*, they said.'

Would any of our boys escape out of HMS something? *Active, Alacrity, Ambuscade, Andromeda, Antelope, Antrim, Ardent, Argonaut, Arrow, Avenger.*

'Is he dangerous?'

'Do Not Approach, the police said. They left a number to ring in case he does pitch up here. And a number for a locksmith to fix the door. Where they just barged in—'

'Argy-bargy.'

'What? But I'm not going down to the phone box until morning. No way. Not in the dark with some murderer about.'

'I've just walked up from there, well, from the bus stop anyway – I managed to get the last bus back, only by the skin of my teeth. Anyway, there's no one down there. Not even Radiation Man.'

'He could be lurking in the shadows.'

'Who? Radiation Man?'

'No, this murderer.'

'Are you as chicken as soup?'

'Just common sense, girl – you want to think about getting some.'

'Well, you won't get a locksmith this time of night.'

On that, they agreed, so between them, they carried Petra's old steamer trunk up the stairs and wedged it behind the front door. It wouldn't stop a really determined axe-murdering crazy from getting in, but it would make plenty of noise coming back down the stairs.

'Who the hell d'you think he is?' asked Stan as they lugged it up.

'Dave,' she said.

Another New Word Enters the Lexicon

The final operational phase of the Falklands War involved considerable hardship for the men who marched long distances across inhospitable terrain in abysmal weather. Some said afterwards, if they could have changed one single thing, they would have had better boots.

David Keane was ex-military, a bruiser with a buzz cut, fanatical about order, extreme fitness, discipline. He permanently maintained battle-ready condition as a matter of pride – even after his dishonourable discharge (1978). He carried on as if nothing had changed. You'd see him in camouflage running up the Wells Road out to the forest. You'd see him coming back, splashed with mud, scratched by brambles, back soaked with sweat. He had a council flat on Faraday Walk. His own private barracks. No comforts: camp bed, stove, CB radio. Kitbag packed and ready to go at a moment's notice. Always waiting for further orders. No one to give him orders. Only the voices in his head. Crazy. Rogue male, survivalist, mercenary, vigilante, a dog of war.

Before, people kept their distance, looked askance. After, after what he did, they called him a hero.

~

Can a man like that adapt to prison regime? Maybe. He liked discipline, respected authority. But he thought they were all soft, the lags and the screws; prison was mollycoddle. But he kept his head down. Then he heard the news. Bad news. BRITISH LION – KILLED WITH PANTS DOWN!* or so the papers said. Held his breath. More lions were lost. One was his brother. Official notification came. Went AWOL. Absconded, they said, and they drew circles on a map, five-mile radius, twenty-mile radius. How far could a man on foot get in an hour? In a day?

After a week, the authorities had to admit they had no idea where he was. No intel, no sightings, no known associates. Of course, they checked his last known address. The distance to home was 152 miles. Portsmouth Harbour, a further 160 miles or so.

Yomp: your own marching pace.

---

*'BRITISH LION – KILLED WITH PANTS DOWN!', *The Guardian*, 1982.

The Balcony

Balcony (noun): From the Italian, balcone *(scaffold). A structural support or executioner's frame. See also* The Balcony, *a play by Jean Genet. Set in a high-class brothel, Genet explores the nature of established societal order and external threats of a revolutionary uprising.*

Sycorax is out cold on brandy, lying on the settee, vast and flaccid in a stained pastel petticoat. DO NOT DISTURB. Everything is going to plan, Callum's plan. He is a genius. GENIUS! Shhhh. Slip out quietly. Her flabby arm flops down, she sighs contentedly like a sow rolling on another piglet. Outside, beyond the shelter of the concrete walkway, rain falls in relentless grey curtains. The air is full of the smell of summer rain on tarmac and pissed-on concrete, the smell of bin bags left out too early or too late, spewing chicken wings and nappies. Everyone is shut in behind grubby doors, or else down the pub, watching the football – tonight is the first of England's World Cup group matches. Having given the Argies a good spanking in the South Atlantic, spirits are high, patriotism is endemic, and England stands poised to conquer the world, even if it is only a game.

Callum stands and listens. He hears nothing but rain and the distant sounds of the city. Nothing moves. He exhales with a snort. He has the big kitchen knife hidden in his anorak sleeve and a mantra: I am a CLEVER BASTARD.

Stop. Out of the corner of his eye, he sees something. On the ground. Crouched close to the wall. Camouflaged, mottled khaki green against the dark wet concrete. He flinches with revulsion. A toad. The wet weather makes them bold; they come from the ditches, up the dark, dank stairwells. Slimy, filthy thing. Then he remembers he is hard as nails. Like Keane. A hero. Like Keane. He skirts past the toad with his back to the wall and turns the corner. Quietly down the steps, one hand lightly skimming the wet metal handrail. From the half landing where the stairs turn, he can see onto next door's balcony, where Keane used to live, before. Before he killed Villiers, before someone grassed him up, before he went to prison, before Callum's jaw got broken, before the posh twats moved in. Students, with their showy ways, thinking they are all that. They are nothing.

He studies their balcony. Water drips from above onto a deckchair, its red striped canvas flapping wetly in the dark. He has seen her there, the little slut in clickety heels, sunning herself. Seen him too, the gawky boy waving his arms and shouting about cat shit. They shit everywhere, dirty cats. No soil to dig proper toilets, just shit on concrete. From the half landing, he can climb onto the parapet and drop onto the balcony. He has seen the kids do it, the skinny ones that hang around, spying, spitting, calling out, catcalling, calling him names. The top flats are all the same; there's a glazed door between the living room and the balcony. The locks on all the balcony doors are weak. Everyone knows that. He can shove his way in, easy-peasy, hunker down in the dark, waiting till she comes home in her clickety-clickety heels. Hear her coming a mile off.

He's on the parapet now, inching along. It's further to fall than he expected, so he avoids looking down. To steady his nerves, he repeats to himself: CLEVER BASTARD, cunning, cunning, cunning.

Shit.

A dim light. Someone is in there, someone sitting in an armchair just behind the glass door, sitting with their legs stuck out. Not her, not the little slut. Not the other one neither, gawky boy with the sticky-up hair, he went out ages ago with his kitbag slung over his shoulder, 'See you tomorrow,' he shouted to her, and 'Take care!'

Who? A man. The man leans forward and begins to unlace his boots.

Shit. Callum watches transfixed as the person he fears most, fears more even than he fears his mother, kicks off his boot, sits up, runs a hand over his shaved head from nape to crown and back to nape, yawns, scratches his belly, and settles back down, making himself at home.

Dave Keane.

He should be in prison. Should be locked up and miles away. Must have got out somehow. How in hell? And why in the fire pits of hell come here? Of all places, why come here? Has Keane come back to get Callum? To get even? Even though Callum didn't do that thing they said he did? Callum's hand gripping the kitchen knife is damp with sweat, his skin clammy and sour, his guts turn to writhing hoses, their contents rank and runny, his sphincter flutters, and his heart yammers in the desolate cavity of his chest. He inches back the way he came. Fumbles back into the safety of the stairwell, retraces his steps along Faraday Walk to the pus-yellow door. Before he slips back in, into the stale fug of his mother's sty, he takes out his weapon, the blade glinting in the flickering sodium light, and with a surprising turn of speed for one so badly made, he lunges and jabs brutally at his new and unwary target.

The blade is not particularly sharp, but it explodes into the body of the toad, rips through and out the other side. It prangs into the pre-cast concrete of the walk, jarring him from fist to collar bone. CLEVER BASTARD.

Buenos Aires, June 1982

I cannot sleep. Sheets like shrouds.

In my dreams, tinned fish, men in metal rooms, cabins, galleys, ships ploughing, drifting. Ships and tankers, submarines skulking in oceans, in depths and shallows. Inside and outside exclusion zones; does it matter? Does it fucking matter? Tinned men, cooked alive, packed in brine. Men floating to the surface, scorched skin, opaque eyes.

Get up, walk the streets.

Winter now in Buenos Aires, and cold, but not fucking cold. I will never feel cold here again.

Silvio's is open, still open. The light spills out into the alley. Silvio glances up, then turns his back on me. The others watch the football. Old men with necks cricked to see a television mounted too high. Football World Cup. This is what matters now. They watch the first of the group matches, France letting the *bastardos Ingléses* walk over them.* I sit at a table, get out my pouch of tobacco, papers, matches, place them on the table, line them up. England is drawn in group three, Argentina in group four; the two adversaries will not meet. Not there.

---

*England defeat France 3–0 in Bilbao but will later be knocked out of the second round following a 0–0 draw with West Germany. Argentina will also be eliminated in the second round, losing to both Brazil and Italy. In the final, Italy will play West Germany and win the tournament 3–1.

'You were there?' Ernesto asks me, his drooping eyelids hitching up a fraction. '*Las Malvinas*?'

'No. Not there.'

Gomez grunts and nudges Ernesto in the ribs. Shut up.

Homecoming Queen

Fear: guts churning with Sauvignon Blanc and bile, piss leaking, mascara running. Petra fumbles and jabs at the lock with her key. Ears straining for a sound beyond her own heart pounding and her anxious breath coming in shallow gasps and sobs. She is listening for that heavy tread, the rant of random threats and obscenities that have so spooked her. At last, the key turns in the lock and the blue door swings inwards. She lurches forward and slams it behind her; she crouches to the floor in despair and relief.

Lock the door.

She limps down two flights of stairs on a twisted ankle and goes first into the bathroom. She lowers herself onto the toilet, pees, touches the dampness of her pants, feels the ragged skin and blood oozing from her knee. Her hand travels down, fingering the swelling, the bruise of her instep; it will be black and blue tomorrow. She eases off her heels: *four* inches of patriarchal subjugation. Feet blistered, skin tabs flapping over red-raw flesh. Ouch.

A disastrous night. Now, alone, she cries from self-pity. She puts on an old sweater from the laundry basket. So absolutely disastrous. Too much to drink, a row with Julian, the 'wine frigging merchant' who turned out to be a complete and utter self-opinionated catalogue-posing arse. He was patronising. She stormed out. Once out on the pavement, she realised she had left her jacket behind. She had hardly any money and couldn't afford a taxi. She ran for the bus, fell over and saw the bus, the *last* bus, pull away from the kerb – without her. Fuelled by both pride and shame, she walked all the way home in the rain, head down, shoulders hunched, arms folded tight against her chest. Not because she was cold but because she felt exposed. After the first mile, she realised she was being followed by a drunken psycho, pitching, ranting, threatening to fuck her with the not particularly phallic trophy he carried, a silver cup glinting under the streetlights. She should have listened to Celeste. Should have got one of those pepper sprays.

Check the door is locked.

His threats reverberate in her head.

'You's all the same, the fucking same. Stuck-up little trollops, pretty boys and perverts. Thinks the world owes you one, thinks you's better than me. Bullseye! Better than us that lives here. It's our city. Frigging cunt scum, nancy-boy dreamers and pencil squeezers with yer lah-di-dah ways. Fuck off back to where you came from. Fucking Surry or Sussex. Little bitches. Cut yer titties off.'

She could smell the booze on him, the sweat, the odour of neglect. Phlegm rattled in his great barrelled chest; drool spilled down his badger-grizzled chin. There was scorn and hate in his hooded eyes. Petra felt sickened by his soiled coat, his lank long hair, and intimidated by his hands like shovels.

'Fucking students. Ha! Stick my cock in yer earhole, carve me name in yer little-bitch lily-white skin. Cut yer little titties off.'

Together, they climbed up the Wells Road, together they passed all the dark places, the derelict parts of the city, its fissures and crevices, onwards and upwards as it sprawled and sputtered out to the margins. Petra in front, him just a few paces behind, shouting his filth. Together they passed the phone box, last outpost of civilization before Lovelace Flats. It was empty, its sickly light flickering. Beyond the flats, the ridge and the new bypass, a no man's land of ditches and vermin and predators. Then the forest.

She glanced over her shoulder, saw him fling back his coat flaps, unzip his flies. With a yelp, she broke into a trot. He had stopped to piss.

Check the door is locked.

Killer Queen

Les tocó en suerte un época extraña. (They lived in a strange age.)*

In the bowels of Faraday Walk, Petra wallows in a pool of misery. A faint noise above distracts her: some small object clattering onto still uncarpeted floorboards. She stiffens. Holds her breath, purses her lips like a blowfish, pufferfish, exhales, and then, exhausted and stoic as to her fate, she inches towards the source of the noise. Up one flight of stairs, and with an outstretched trepid finger, she opens the living room door...

What she will find is a lean and dirty man. Not the man she is afraid of; this one is much younger and not ranting. He's slumped in a chair near the balcony door, one boot off and a syringe sticking into his foetid foot, between his toes, in between the piggy that went to market and the one that stayed at home. His eyelids are half shut, head thrown back, exposing his throat, as if he re-enacts the Ecstasy of the Magdalene.

When she sees him, Petra will be startled, then annoyed. Instead of the screaming panic an intruder might occasion, what she will feel, after the initial shock, is *annoyance*: something else to ruin her night, something else to sort out, more mess. A fucking corpse. He is dead, obviously, a dead junkie

---

*'Juan López y John Ward' by Jorge Luis Borges.

sprawled in Stan's armchair. The balcony door is slightly ajar, and the night air is cool and damp after the rain. She will approach quietly. Should she check his pulse? A formality, but just to be sure. Or look for a wallet, something with a name? She will crouch down and study him. Sallow skin, more than stubble, a straggly beard of a week or more, ingrained dirt, cracked lips, probably been living rough, tattoos on his neck and his hands, long strings of numbers and symbols like algebra or maybe—

'Ohhh!'

He tenses, lurches, gasps, and slumps back as if punched. Not dead.

Now. *Now* Petra panics. Oh, fuck. Oh, shitting fuckety-fuck-fuck. He's alive, still breathing. What to do? Junkie. Overdose. Keep him awake. Pull the needle out? Blanket, keep him warm, adrenaline, they jab them with adrenaline, slap his face? Recovery position, blanket, anaphylactic fuck shock, fuck ambulance.

To ring for an ambulance, she must leave the flat and walk in the dark down the road to the phone box. She is afraid to leave the flat. At last, Petra is afraid. Afraid because of what is outside. That man. This man, his chest rising fractionally, breaths shallow and infrequent. He needs help.

At the phone box, the old derelict with the five hundred metres swimming trophy will still be staggering in the road, shouting abuse, waiting for his chance to cut her titties off. He's old but still strong, more than capable of dragging her into the bushes to rape and mutilate her. She can feel his calloused hands, smell the stale fags and sour whiskey vomit of his breath, smell the musty twill of his stained trousers, taste the flap of his overcoat as he swallows her into his unspeakable violent fantasy. Her skin crawls as he unzips his flies, pulls out his festering cock and pisses on her, then with his pocketknife, carves his name in her flesh.

Perhaps the next-door neighbours have a phone?

Petra looks out of her door, left towards the piss-stinking stairwell, and right, down the length of the walk. Nothing. Nothing moves. Leaving her scuzzy blue door on the latch, she knocks tentatively on the rancid-butter yellow of Number 39. Eventually, there's a muffled sound of footsteps, and the door opens a fraction.

'Er, I live next door—'

'I know.'

'Could I use your phone?'

The man looks at her. He has a broad pockmarked face like an underripe strawberry and full jammy lips. He is wearing an anorak as if he was just going out or just coming in. Petra has seen him outside the Nightjar, hanging around, muttering to himself. Strange that after living here for months, she didn't know he was her neighbour. He keeps looking at her, vacant, haunted. Learning difficulties, she thinks.

'No.'

'Please. I need to ring for an ambulance.'

He shifts uneasily, repositioning something behind his back. And licks his lips.

'No. I mean, we ain't got no phone.'

She studies his face as if to detect a lie. He is clammy under her gaze, his mouth twitching as if in spasm. Then he turns abruptly. She catches a glint of the blade behind his back as he kicks the yellow door shut.

Deflated, she limps back in through the blue door. Her junkie is still there, still breathing. She sits on the floor by the balcony door, hugging her knees. Her ankle aches, blistered feet stink. She rocks back and forth, weeping for herself, for being put in such an intolerable position. Scared to go out, scared to stay in.

He is still; she touches him. Touches the surprisingly pale skin of his throat, and he sighs, all but imperceptibly. She kneels beside him.

'Dave,' she says, almost a whisper.

'Dave,' and she shakes his arm but gets no response.

~

In his messed-up head, *she* doesn't exist; he is running, ploughing through banks of nettles, leaping over ditches, he can feel the wind, he is pushing the pace, heading south, running to his brother. She explains why she hasn't called an ambulance, and he hears none of it.

Home at last, Dave Keane, lone wolf, loner, local hero. Never tried skag until he went to prison, and he found it hushed the voices in his head. Surprisingly easy to get hold of – inside and outside. He has yomped cross-country a long way, still a long way to go. In four more days, maybe five, he will reach Portsmouth, wait for the coffin ships, wait for what remains to be shipped home.† But the stuff in his veins is poison, and while Petra weeps, her pretty face blotched and streaked with dirt and snot, Keane dies. The moon rises in the sky behind them, lighting the room, casting shadows.

†Alex Keane was buried at sea in the Falkland Sound.

Epilogue: Toads Singing A Cappella

Hush. Listen to the treacle tarmac contracting and re-solidifying as the heat of another day fades. An ice-cream van, as if observing curfew, trundles home with a last tinkling flurry. Encased in shoddy concrete, the inhabitants of three hundred and forty flats bicker and fuck. They tell lies, fry eggs, watch *Countdown*, wipe arses, iron shirts, take painkillers, and bemoan the state of the nation or the kitchen. Below them, in the Nightjar, Kenneth wipes pint glasses with a dirty cloth, and further down the Wells Road, in the suburbs, they watch the television news and sport, cheering victory from the vantage of armchairs. Further down still, the city hums in a veil of dust. Its sparkling, seedy, old money, enterprising commercial heart still beats. It has survived so much: plague, famine, crusaders, bombers, boom and bust. A place of obdurate resilience.

But look uphill. Look beyond the flats and the used and broken ground to a stony ridge, a bypass under construction, and beyond that, the forest. Once, it was a vast deciduous ocean, but centuries of human progress have diminished it. Yet like the city, its heartwood endures, a watchful fortress crisscrossed by a thousand lonely paths. Dave Keane used to pound along those paths, counting, sweat-dripping, muttering, obsessive and peculiar. From Lovelace Flats, as you open wide the steel-framed pivot windows to throw your rubbish out, you might, if you listen, detect the faintest moaning of the trees as they stretch and sway, hear the drum of his feet on the ground, or you might hear the glorious sound of toads in dry ditches, singing a cappella.

GAME OVER

ACKNOWLEDGEMENTS

Thanks must go first to Michael Loveday and to David Rhymes who gave incisive editorial feedback and generous encouragement when I needed it most. Thanks also to David Borrowdale and Reflex Press for publishing this and for unstinting promotion of the beautiful form of flash fiction. Thanks to all at the Open University who have been so supportive, especially Jane, Charly, Bridget, Kay, Kathy, Christine, and Reg. Special thanks to Maya Jordan for keeping me on the path and out of the woods, and to the coven: Holly V. Chilton, Jackie Morris, and Mina Ma for highbrow discussions and lowbrow snark.